THE DATING GAME

Fenella Grant starts a new chapter of her life when she opens her own matchmaking agency. All is going well — until James McAllister's sister buys him a year's membership in an attempt to change his casual dating habits. James has no intention of settling down, and insists Fen cancel his subscription. Instead, she matches him with her most intimidating client. James is furious, then intrigued — who is this elusive woman setting him up with unwanted dates? And why does she refuse to meet him . . . ?

SARAH EVANS

THE DATING GAME

Complete and Unabridged

LINFORD
Leicester

First published in Great Britain in 2008

First Linford Edition
published 2014

A catalogue record for this book is available
from the British Library.

ISBN 978–1–4448–1826–0

Published by
F. A. Thorpe (Publishing)
Anstey, Leicestershire
Set by Words & Graphics Ltd.
Anstey, Leicestershire
Printed and bound in Great Britain by
T. J. International Ltd., Padstow, Cornwall
This book is printed on acid-free paper

Dedication
My Family

Trademark Acknowledgements

Candid Camera, Irving Brecher
Cats, composed by Andrew Lloyd Webber, lyrics by T.S. Eliot and Trevor Nunn
Garfield, United Feature Syndicate
Good King Wenceslas, Jacques Salzedo
Jensen, Jensen Motors Ltd
Lycra, Invista North America S.A.R.L. Corporation
Swan Lake, Peter Ilytich Tchaikovsky
Winnie The Pooh, Walt Disney Company

1

The pealing of the phone pierced the darkened office as James McAllister unlocked the door. He sourly regarded the deserted fifth floor of McAllister Electronics, his breath making frozen clouds in the sub-zero temperature of the high-rise. He thumped down his briefcase and overnight bag and glanced at his watch, grimacing when he read the dial. Four o'clock in the afternoon, but his body told him it was the middle of the night.

The sound of freezing sleet hitting the window reached his ears. Typical December weather. James rubbed a hand over his tired eyes. He was jetlagged and chilled to the core. All he wanted to do was go home to the peaceful sanctuary of his comfortable apartment. There it would be warm and silent and far from the madding pre-Christmas crowds that had made traveling so darn difficult. But however much he wanted to shut out the world under a scalding shower, ridding himself of travel grime and tiredness, it wasn't an option. He had a date.

He also had to answer the wretched phone, which still rang with strident persistence and aggravated his throbbing head with a vengeance.

He hit the light switch. Nothing. Well, the lack of power didn't affect the phone, more's the pity. In the gloom, James made for the phone but tripped over an unsuspecting chair and hit his shin on its black metal leg. Sharp pain gave an added, instant dimension to the duller ache in his head and made James mutter a dark curse against the unknown caller causing all his grief. He hopped about, holding his smarting shin. The phone continued ringing. He snatched at the receiver but missed and knocked over the desk light, which caused a neat pile of papers to rustle to the carpet like a snowdrift of windswept flakes.

James growled and finally grabbed the receiver. 'Yes?' He rubbed his shin through the fine wool of his expensive tailored trousers. He wished he were a thousand miles away from this icy, unforgiving environment. Though he was proud of the success of his computer software company, there were times like these when he could happily forgo its responsibilities. If he'd had a conventional nine-to-five job, he'd probably have been married by now and would be thinking of heading home to the cozy warmth of his family rather than standing here in the glacial dark and addressing a faceless, nameless client.

'James McAllister?' The voice on the other end of the line was soft and melodic, but James only lent it half an ear as he tried to straighten the mayhem on the desk in the minimal glow offered by the fire exit sign.

'Speaking.' He righted the desk light and flipped its switch. That didn't work either. Blanket power failure? Brilliant. He'd have been better off staying in New York. At least it hadn't been snowing there.

'Good afternoon, Mr. McAllister, I'm calling from Discreet Liaisons. I wanted to touch base with you, check a few details and request an up-to-date photo for our files.'

'Discreet who?'

'Liaisons.'

'Never heard of you. You must have the wrong number.' Where was Valerie? She was employed to screen crank calls.

'We're a dating agency,' said the woman.

She sounded young and detached, which didn't improve James' temper. He didn't have the patience for a sales pitch by someone too young and inexperienced to care about whatever she was promoting. In fact, he didn't have the patience for a sales pitch, period. He wanted to go home and sleep.

'Definitely a wrong number,' he

clipped out, preparing to hang up.

'You have a year's membership with us.'

James hesitated. 'Is this some sort of joke or selling scam?' he said, his voice wary. 'I have no need to join a dating agency. I don't have to pay to get dates.' What was she on? He'd had people try to sell him time-share apartments and insurance, but dates? He preferred to find his own, thank you very much. Just how did she think she was going to hook him? Offer him a special deal for two? Or maybe a group? Kinky. Perhaps he should find out for the devilment of it, though really he didn't have time. He was going to the theatre and there were numerous things to do before he went out.

'No need to sound so defensive, Mr. McAllister. There's no shame in being lonely and wanting to be pro-active about meeting women. A dating agency is a marvelous way of finding companionship. You meet lots of new people who can enrich your life.'

Though usually an even-tempered person, the woman's inane spiel about dating agencies irritated him. 'Ms. Whoever-you-are . . . ?'

'Grant. Fenella Grant.'

'Ms. Grant, I do not have to resort to an agency. I have many women friends, plenty of companionship and I don't need my life enriched any further.' Especially since he'd been introduced into the modeling world through a business associate. The experience offered him a rich and varied selection of dates and, though enjoyable, his social life was complicated enough without tossing another load of strange women into the equation. Dating gorgeous women without commitment suited his busy lifestyle. But who knew what would be served up through a dating agency? He shuddered to think.

'I'm sure you *think* you're leading a fulfilled life,' said Fenella in a low, soothing voice. 'But on your membership form you've stated you haven't had any long-term, stable relationships in almost two decades.'

Fenella's tone irritated James. It reminded him of his mother and his sister, or any woman, when they wished him to do something he really, really didn't want to. Once upon a time it was employed to cajole him to eat his brussel sprouts — *just one more, Jamie, because they're really good for you*. Or used when telling him to partner a friend of the family's social pariah daughter to a debutant function so no one felt sorry for her. They'd never thought of his own tender teenage feelings. Those sort of reasonable, modulated, we-know-best-for-you tones gave him the heebie-jeebies. They were downright dangerous and he wasn't going to be sucked in by them this time round.

'What? Who told you? This is ridiculous! I haven't filled in any membership forms. I'd never even heard of your sad little agency until two minutes ago.'

She tripped on, ignoring him. 'Lack

of commitment can be due to low self-esteem.'

James swore and was about to break the connection when he thought he heard a giggle. Hah, so she thought this was funny, did she?

'Though of course,' continued Fenella, 'Using that sort of language when talking to women explains why you've had to resort to using our agency.'

'There is nothing wrong in the way I treat women. I've had no complaints so far.' James' blood pressure rose. Ms. Grant was proving an exception to the rule. He wanted to throttle her!

'Bombastic, boorish behavior doesn't go down well in our enlightened and empowered feminist society,' said Fenella.

The woman had to be kidding. James loosened his tie and shirt collar. His jetlag must be worse than he'd thought. He pinched the bridge of his nose between his forefinger and thumb and squeezed shut his scratchy, dry eyes. Perhaps he was hallucinating due to exhaustion? Women usually found him attractive. He was successful, personally wealthy, and generous to those he cared about. He'd never been accused of being bombastic and boorish.

'One has to be sensitive to a woman's needs if one wants to gain her respect,' Fenella carried on. 'I tell you what, how about I book you into some self-improvement classes so you can work on your communication skills? You might then be able to form proper relationships.'

'Enough!' James grappled to keep a lid on his temper by clenching his jaw and taking a long, slow breath. He didn't want to give Ms. Grant the satisfaction of a bout of bombastic, boorish behavior. 'You've gone too far. I'm perfectly able to communicate with any normal, *reasonable* person.'

'Really, these courses are extremely beneficial for those who suffer from short temper. They can be tremendous fun and liberate you from all that extra personal baggage you've been carting about for years which has prevented you from forming long-lasting attachments.'

'You speak from experience, I suppose,' said James, goaded by her patronizing tone. He was tempted to end the call, but he didn't want to give her the satisfaction of thinking she was right.

'You're being defensive again, Mr. McAllister.'

'Let's get this straight. I have not joined your agency. I want nothing to do with your pathetic little feel-good courses. And I don't want to hear from you again. Clear?'

'Okay.'

She sounded too perky for James' liking. What was going on? She should be back-pedaling by now.

'I'll concede that you didn't pay for the membership.'

'Good.'

'But someone did, so you might as well take advantage of our services.'

James' knuckles whitened their hold on the receiver as he grappled with his temper. 'Never,' he said shortly.

'May I just check some facts?' Fenella didn't wait for his consent. She read out his birth date.

James swore again. The woman just didn't get it, did she? He wanted nothing to do with the agency.

'There's no need to be shy about your age. We have a big demand for the more mature man. And forty is — '

James was sure her hesitation was a deliberate attempt to stifle her laughter.

' — quite a prime age, really, you know, for some people.'

'I have no problem with being forty,' he said with a snap that threatened to shatter his jawbone.

'I'm so glad, Mr. McAllister. A lot of middle-aged men feel extremely sensitive about their passing years and forty is, let's face it, such a *significant* landmark.'

James heard the giggle again, and his temper flared hotter. He had better things to do than sit in a freezing, blacked-out office on a late Friday afternoon talking to this nutty woman. 'Delete my name and details from your files and do not contact me again.'

'I'm afraid it's too late to cancel your first date. It's already scheduled.'

'That's your problem. I'm not in the market for sex-starved singletons.'

'Lucinda is thirty-six, divorced, with no children. She has her own travel agency in the city, and she'll be contacting you very shortly.'

'Ms. Grant!'

'Your form states you can be the ultimate gentleman. I'm relying on you to live up to that statement. Even in these enlightened times, a woman needs courage to ask a man out. Lucinda is vulnerable. Be nice to her.'

'Don't bank on it!'

'Oh, and Mr. McAllister. Happy birthday.'

James heard the beginnings of a chuckle, followed by an abrupt click, terminating the call. He ran his hand through his hair. That woman was a menace. He glared at the phone. How had she got his name and number? Obviously from someone who knew him well, which begged the question: which one of his family and friends had set him up? He was determined to find out as soon as possible. In the meantime, what was he doing about this date?

★   ★   ★

Fen replaced the telephone receiver and burst out laughing. James McAllister hadn't heard the last of her, not by any stretch of the imagination. His sister, Belle, who paid for the birthday membership, made it clear she wanted Fen to set him up with a good selection of women. She felt James needed lightening up. In Belle's opinion, he was too serious, too hard-working and had the dreadful habit of serially dating unsuitable women. Belle wanted to shake him up, maybe get him thinking of settling down and having a family with a nice, *suitable* girl.

Fen typed Lucinda's details into the

computer and watched the information come up on the screen and giggled again. Lucinda was a lovely lady, but vulnerable she was not. Fen doubted if she knew the meaning of the word. When Lucinda had first signed up, she'd actually asked for an alphabetic listing of all the available men on Fen's files. Lucinda was also a dab hand at asking out men. James McAllister may find that he was the vulnerable one when he came face-to-face with Lucinda Burton.

Fen had lied about the scheduled date too. She hadn't set up anything. Yet. But she would, and straight away before common sense kicked in. She e-mailed Lucinda James' details, embellishing where appropriate, and then e-mailed Belle to say they were on track.

That done, she stared at her computer screen for a good five minutes, debating with herself. James McAllister piqued her interest. She remained detached from most of her clients, but he was something a little different. Correction, a lot different. He wasn't the usual lonely male looking for a little loving company. If he and his sister were to be believed, he had an over-supply of girlfriends. More importantly, he'd made her laugh. Not something that happened much these days. So would it hurt to have a little look again at his records?

Her hand hovered over the mouse. She shouldn't, really. Strictly no involvement with clients was Discreet Liaisons' number one rule. But as she had written the rules herself, she was well within her rights to bend or break them. She could research anyone she liked, when she liked.

Fen pulled up his file on the computer screen and scrolled down the information. On the face of it, the profile was impressive. But his sister must have exaggerated. No man could be this good. Belle had said he ran his own computer software business which involved overseas travel. He was also sporty, easygoing and generous.

Fen shook her head and grimaced. He hadn't sounded terribly easygoing on the phone. Downright grouchy in fact, what with all the growling and bluster.

She read Belle's physical description of her brother and took it with a healthy dollop of salt. He was apparently a shade under six feet, brown-haired and gray-eyed. The description was too generic. A photo would have been much nicer because then she could have studied it. Not because she was interested. Of course not. She didn't want a relationship at all. But her curiosity had *definitely* been piqued.

A few clicks and she closed down her computer, and then grimaced at the open curtains. Outside the night was pitch black and forbidding. Sleet pelted the window. Fen shivered. What a miserable Friday evening, and not only because she had nothing to do tonight except lie on the floor and run through her exercises, vegetate in the armchair in front of the television and then go to bed, to hopefully sleep, if the pain allowed.

She hauled herself to her feet, waited until she felt centered and then slowly maneuvered her way across the room, holding on to pieces of strategically placed furniture. In the house, Fen tried her hardest not to use the crutches. She was determined to walk unaided wherever possible. Small beginnings. The longest journey started with one step, right?

At the window she stared into the wet blackness. Rush hour cars streamed past, sheeting icy water onto the pavements. Fen shivered again and yanked the curtains shut to block out the disturbing scene.

On a similar freezing, sleety night the previous year, she'd been involved in a hit-and-run accident while out jogging. She'd been left for dead. On her blackest days, Fen wondered if she'd have been better off dead rather than living this pain-filled half-life.

Fen abruptly turned away and gritted her teeth against the sharp pain in her left hip. Slowly she let out her breath as the stabbing hurt receded to a dull ache. She eased herself forward, more carefully this time, and headed toward her small kitchen. She'd make a cup of tea and knock up some pasta for dinner, do her exercise routine and then eat. Focus on doing, not thinking. Focus on living, not lying in a streaming gutter half-dead.

While waiting for the kettle to boil, Fen practiced some basic ballet limbering up exercises, gritting her teeth against the pain. Before the accident, she'd been a dancer on the brink of an international career. She'd appeared in the musicals *Cats* and *Queen*. Now she was pushed to put one foot in front of the other without falling in a heap or doubling up in agony.

With determination, she finished her quota just as her phone rang. She let the answer phone pick up as she pushed herself to do a few more exercises, mentally counting her bends and breaths.

'Fenella? Lucinda, hi. Got your message. Can't wait to fix up this McAllister bloke. Is he the McAllister of McAllister Electronics? Hope so. Will let you know how I go. Bye for now.'

Fen grinned and did a couple more knee bends. Lucky McAllister. He was in for a very special treat.

* * *

James was ticked off as he trudged through acres of offices and miles of silent corridors. Everyone in the multi-story building seemed to have disappeared. He'd even had difficultly rousing security, finding the men huddled around a portable gaslight, drinking takeaway coffee and playing cards. The approaching Christmas holiday was no excuse for staff to grow slack.

As he made his way back to his office, he flicked a glance at his watch.

He was running late thanks to the irritating Ms. Grant of Discreet Liaisons. Squinting in the gloom, he rang his secretary at her home. 'Where the hell is everyone, Valerie?' he demanded. 'Why has the building been evacuated? It's not Christmas yet, you know.'

'Calm down, James,' said Valerie Lucas peaceably. 'We were told the power would be off all day and with no heating or computers, I gave everyone a day off to save them the hassle of going on strike.'

'I see. So you're telling me I should be grateful?'

'Yes, even if you don't sound it.'

'I don't like the office unstaffed during work hours.'

'Neither do I, so I stayed answering the phones until mid-afternoon. By then the place was so cold and miserable I was in danger of suffering frostbite. I decided I'd done my bit for Queen, McAllister and country and went home too.'

'Okay, you're forgiven. That was

beyond the call of duty.' James relied on his secretary one hundred percent. She'd been with him since the beginning of his business and often deputized for him while he traveled overseas.

'Thank you. I take it I can have a Christmas bonus?'

'You always do, dear Valerie.' He gave a short laugh and then said, 'Do you know anything about Discreet Liaisons?'

'Are you suggesting we have an affair, James? I didn't know you fancied older women. Or is that my bonus?'

'Discreet Liaisons is a dating agency,' James growled in frustration.

She chuckled. 'I know.'

'I see. Joke. I'm *really* in the mood for them at this precise moment. So, have you used the agency?'

'No, but it has a good reputation. It's not your call girl type of affair as far as I understand it. Why, are you thinking of signing up? Have you finally run out of women? Dear me, not a good thing to happen with your big four-O birthday and the festive season upon us.' She chuckled again.

James experienced another wave of irritation towards Ms. Grant, who'd started this whole thing. 'Thank you, Val,' he said with a touch of exasperation. 'I'll deal with you on Monday.'

After ringing off, James hefted up his briefcase and overnight bag and locked the office, leaving it in darkness. Taking a taxi home, he had a lightning quick shower and got into his tux just as his date arrived. Chrissy was a model and a friend of one of his business associates. She looked great and was undemanding, which suited James admirably. But tonight he wasn't in the mood to be sociable. He just wanted to go to bed and sleep.

As he opened the door and greeted Chrissy with a perfunctory kiss, the phone rang.

'Ignore it, darling,' said Chrissy. 'Or we'll be late.'

'I'm expecting a business call.' James

whisked up the receiver and rattled off the number.

'Now that's what I call one very sexy voice,' said a woman with the low throaty drawl of a serious smoker.

'Excuse me?'

'I'm after James McAllister?'

An awful premonition hit James. 'Speaking.'

'I'm Lucinda Burton. Darling Fen told me you're a real cracker. Can't wait to meet you.'

'*Darling* Fen got it all wrong, I'm afraid. Ms. Burton, I'm not in the market for blind dates.'

A husky laugh wafted down the phone and curled around James. 'Honey, there's nothing wrong with my eyesight and I can't wait to get an eyeful of you. Now don't be shy. I understand it's your first time, so I'll be gentle. How about we meet on neutral territory to make you feel more comfortable?'

James made a choking sound of disbelief. Hadn't Ms. Grant said this woman was vulnerable? No way! He could hear the sultry confidence oozing down the phone. He'd met the type before: pushy and predatory. He always did his damnedest to avoid them.

'How about the Talisman Club in Tottenham Court Road? Eight tomorrow night suit you?' she breathed.

'You're wasting your time.'

'Let me be the judge of that, sugar.'

'I won't be there.'

'Fen said you'd need plenty of coaxing and, honey, I'm the one to coax a man. I'll see you at eight. Don't disappoint me now.' The phone clicked off.

James stared in disbelief at the phone. 'She can't be serious.'

'Who?' said Chrissy.

'Lucinda. And that Grant woman.' James snatched up the telephone directory and began flicking through the yellow pages. He'd give Fenella Grant a piece of his mind. He refused to be steamrolled into this dating game.

'James, we're already late.' The young

24

woman pouted and tugged at the sleeve of his jacket.

James glanced at his watch. Chrissy was right. They'd be lucky to make it for the first act. He ripped the relevant pages from the directory and stuffed them into his jacket pocket. He'd scan the numbers later and ring her from the theatre. He would not be beaten.

Fifteen minutes in, the play failed to hold James' interest. The yellow pages were burning a hole in his pocket. He was twitching to find Fenella Grant's number and give her a blast. No way would he meet this Lucinda Burton. He was not someone to go on blind dates with man-eaters. Quietly as possible, he withdrew the paper from his jacket.

Chrissy frowned at him.

James unfolded the pages with a crackle.

Chrissy's frown deepened.

James, obsessed with finding the number so he could ring it as soon as intermission arrived, tried to straighten out the sheets and angle them so he could read them in the half-light of the stage. Darn it, Discreet Liaisons wasn't listed. Sighing in frustration, he scrunched up the paper into a tight ball, which won him another rash of furious stares from the surrounding patrons.

That was it. He was out of here. He couldn't concentrate on the play. Even without the mental irritation of Ms. Grant, the drama was too modern and arty for his liking. 'I'll see you in the bar,' he whispered to Chrissy and escaped the auditorium before she could stop him.

From the public booth in the bar, James rang directory inquires and got the agency's number. He dialed and the phone rang for a while. He fully expected an answering service to kick in. No matter if it did. The need to vent his spleen churned his stomach. He was ready to record some pretty pithy remarks to Ms. Grant, but the phone kept ringing.

James was just about to hang up

when a woman's breathless voice answered. He'd been primed to blast his outrage but she sounded as if someone had already given her a physical battering.

Her breaths were coming in short, sharp, pain-filled gasps that rasped down the phone line.

'Ms. Grant? Fenella? Are you okay?' Stupid question. Her ragged sigh sounded as if she was in agony.

'Yes.'

'You don't sound okay. Shall I call a doctor? An ambulance? Tell me where you are and I'll come and help.' He felt useless, stuck here at the theater, when she was in such need.

'It's nothing I can't handle. Who is this?' she whispered.

'James McAllister.'

Silence.

'Are you still there?'

'Yes. What do you want?' Her voice lacked the brisk bounciness of her earlier call.

'Get Lucinda Burton off my back.'

His words came out without fire, his anger evaporating at the pitiful sound of her suffering.

'Okay, whatever. Consider it done.'

He found her frailty disturbing. James much preferred her perky teasing, however annoying it had been initially.

'Are you sure you're all right?' He expected her to laugh, to challenge him to see the date through to the end. Her lack of fight unnerved him. What was wrong with the woman? 'Have you been attacked?'

'No.'

The catch in her voice shafted him in the gut. 'Then what?' he asked, but her reply was lost in the rush and din of people crowding into the bar after the first act. 'Sorry, I didn't hear that. What did you say?'

'There's a lot of noise at your end.'

'I'm at the theater. It's the interval. I'll call you back in a few minutes when it's quieter.'

'No! Please! Not tonight.'

She sounded desperate, the panicked edge to her voice slicing through him and causing his stomach to clench. 'Tomorrow morning, then. Ring me if you need me before that. Promise me that you will, whatever the time.' He gave her his mobile phone number, repeating it three times to make sure she'd written it down correctly before he rang off. He didn't like breaking the connection. She sounded much too vulnerable. But what else could he do?

He tugged at his collar and then ran a distracted hand through his hair. For the first time in years James was at a loss. He slammed his hand against the phone booth in frustration, but it did nothing to alleviate his sense of inadequacy.

2

Fen stared at the phone long and hard. Now what was that all about? Why had McAllister The Arrogant suddenly come on as Sir Caring Knight in shining armor, wanting to gallop to her supposed rescue? He'd been ready to string her up on the gallows earlier in the day. Had she really sounded so bad he'd thought she'd been attacked? So much for her brilliant telephone manner. It needed some good, sound polishing.

She flicked on the answering machine. She expected her mother to call, but the machine could pick it up. Fen would ring her back tomorrow, when she felt more rested. Leaning heavily on her crutches, Fen slowly limped her way to the bedroom. It was only a matter of time before the painkillers kicked in and then she'd be able to sleep. Well, that was the theory, anyway. Some nights they worked and some nights they didn't.

She maneuvered her way into bed, plumping up the pillows into strategic places to give her maximum support, and then cuddled under her duvet. As the aching throb eased, she began to relax her limbs. Soon she floated on to dreamland.

A dull thumping thud, thud, thudded in her brain. Fen squished her sleepy eyes shut. That's all she needed, a crashing migraine to add to all her other aches and pains. She'd really overdone the exercises the previous night — all James McAllister's fault. She'd felt so buoyant after setting him up with Lucinda, she'd pushed herself too hard.

Thud, thud, thud.

Hang on? The noise was coming from outside her head. Lord, it was the front door. Who the heck? Fen squinted at her bedside clock. Nine. Not *that* late. But not that early either.

31

The doorbell pealed for far longer than was pleasant. Whoever it was must want to see her urgently. She struggled to her feet and, grabbing hold of doorjambs and furniture, made it to the front door before her visitor had succeeded in pounding it to sawdust.

'Okay, I'm coming, I'm coming,' she called out and then fumbled to unbolt the door.

'You took your time. I was about to ring the police,' growled a complete stranger who glowered menacingly on her doorstep. He was hunched in a bulky black weatherproof jacket and blue jeans. He was much taller than Fen's five-foot-four, and broad-shouldered, though that could have been the coat padding. His nose had appeared to have lost the fight in a rough rugby scrum at some stage in its career. The icy rain pelted down, drenching him and plastering his hair to his head. He had eyes to match the ice. They sparked glacial slithers at Fen and made her shiver from the outside in.

Fen clutched the door hard, partly to support herself and partly to bang it shut if the man turned dangerous. Because he certainly looked dangerous, if the nose was anything to go by.

'What's wrong? Has there been an accident?' She tried to peer around his bulk and this time shivered outwardly as a blast of arctic wind whistled straight through her fleecy pajamas.

'You tell me.' His voice had the cultured clip of an expensive education, but what he was saying didn't make any sense to Fen. She wasn't the one who'd been causing a commotion.

Eek. She had a crazy on her doorstep. Don't panic. But her heart fluttered like a caged canary just the same. 'I'm sorry?' She tried to sound calm and in control but it was hard when one was wearing Garfield PJs while conversing with a large, rain-soaked lunatic.

'I've been worrying about you all night. I've hardly slept a wink,' ground out the nut.

'I'm sorry but I don't know who you

are. I think you'd better leave.' Fen gripped the door tighter, preparing to slam it in his face. 'Or I'll call the police.'

'You are Fenella Grant?'

'I might be,' she hedged, not wanting to give anything away that might damn her later.

'Yes or no?' The words were a barked command from someone used to being obeyed.

But Fen wasn't intimidated. She'd never been good at following orders. 'Who wants to know?' She thrust out her chin and awarded him a gimlet stare.

A flicker of uncertainty swept his rugged features. 'I do. I'm James McAllister.'

James McAllister? Good grief! Fen was tempted to say that she'd never heard of him but that would have been cowardly and craven and she was neither. But she was intrigued.

So this was the serial womanizer with a commitment problem? Not quite what she'd expected, what with the crooked nose and wings of silver at the temples. He appeared all of his forty years, complete with bags around the eyes. What was the big deal? How come he had so many women willing to date him? He was no Mr. Universe.

'Sorry, I suppose I should have introduced myself,' he continued, frowning. 'But I was preoccupied. I thought Ms. Grant might be seriously hurt. When she didn't answer the phone this morning and then nobody answered the door, I imagined the worst.' His words petered out, a crease appeared between his eyes and then he suddenly demanded, 'Are *you* Fenella Grant?' His gaze raked her up and down.

Fen cringed. She was glad the door hid most of her PJ grinning Garfields and bare feet. But what did her hair look like? Definitely mussed after a night of tossing and turning. Were there smudges of mascara under her eyes? Had she dried drool on her chin?

And did those things really matter in the scheme of things? No. But she was irked anyway. She had enough female vanity to want to look good in front of a man, even if the man was James McAllister. 'Yes,' she admitted. 'I'm Fen.'

'Ah, so you haven't been rushed off to hospital or lying helpless on the floor. I'm glad. I've been imagining all manner of terrible fates.' His frown disappeared and he smiled.

Okay, so that smile was the big deal. It changed everything about him. It relieved the tension in his face, lit his gray eyes so they gleamed silver and made him less of a lunatic and more a member of the human race. It also knocked a good few years off his face and those tired bags almost disappeared.

Fen managed to smile back but was still very conscious of her PJs.

'I don't know if you've noticed but it's freezing and wet out here.'

Was that a hint? Did he expect to

come in? Oh no. No way would she allow him to step inside her flat and catch her at her most vulnerable. 'I'm not dressed,' she announced.

James gazed at her pajamas. 'I can wait while you make yourself decent.'

'And I'm really not well enough to receive visitors.' It would take her all of half an hour to limp back to the bedroom, dress and limp back. She couldn't have him lurking about her flat for that long.

He hesitated. 'I'm sorry. I shouldn't be keeping you talking out in the cold. If there's anything you need, cold medicine, chicken broth, brandy, just give me a call.'

'You're very kind.'

'The perfect gentleman,' he said dryly.

'So I read on your form.' Fen's lips twitched.

'Hmm.' He looked as though he would say more, no doubt about his dubious membership of Discreet Liaisons and how he wanted to wriggle off

37

the Lucinda hook, but then changed his mind. Phew, Fen didn't feel able to battle with him this morning.

'I'll be in touch,' he said. 'Get better.'

Fen shut the door. Leaning against it, she blew out a long, heartfelt sigh. That had been an unexpected encounter. She hadn't thought to meet James McAllister quite so soon, if ever. And she was pleased he'd presumed she suffered from the flu. It was refreshing having someone treating her as a normal person rather than pussyfooting around, trying not to upset her.

Since the accident, family and friends had smothered her with love. She didn't doubt their sincerity, but it was cloying all the same. James McAllister wasn't hampered by the pity which had paralyzed her close relationships since the hit-and-run.

The accident had caused multiple injuries, including her legs that had been badly broken. Even her face had had to be reconstructed as her cheekbones had shattered on impact with the pavement. The result had been endless months in hospital with lots of painful surgery and excruciating physiotherapy. Fen had known from the outset her dancing would be a thing of the past, but the fact that walking was a debatable reality had really rattled her.

But she hadn't given up. She'd pig-headedly refused to accept she might never walk again and had embarked on a grueling exercise program. Months down the track, she still couldn't move with the fluid grace of a ballerina, but she could limp along on crutches. It was only a matter of time and endurance before she would be able to throw them away and walk unaided.

★ ★ ★

James skirted puddles to return to his car. He turned up his collar against the driving rain and won himself some icy trickles down his neck. Brilliant. What a horrible day to be out. At least he'd

39

established Fenella Grant wasn't dying, though she'd looked damn close to it with her drawn, frail face and her dark blue eyes so bruised and sad.

He had to admit she wasn't what he'd expected. She stood a good few inches shorter than he'd imagined, probably because he was so used to dating models. Her face was as white and translucent as the petal of an iceberg rose, as if she'd been ill for a long period of time. Her almost black hair had been butchered within an inch of its life and spiked across her skull so she resembled a pixie who'd suffered an electric shock. To be fair, she'd only just fallen out of bed, a fact borne out by those crazy, furry-cat pajamas. He hadn't realized women wore those sorts of things. The women of his acquaintance wore silky, sexy negligees, not get-ups better suited to a kindergarten sleepover.

If Fenella Grant had been in better shape, James would have tackled her about this Lucinda problem. There was no way he wanted to go on the date, because he didn't hold a shred of belief that it would be enjoyable. But there was no method of contacting Lucinda Burton and canceling. Sighing deeply, his breath pluming white around him, James cranked up the engine of his silver Jensen and shunted the heat controls on high. It was time to head for home and catch up on his lack of sleep so he would be in top form to handle the not-so-vulnerable Lucinda Burton.

★ ★ ★

At two minutes to eight James sat in his car with the heater blasting high. He parked outside the Talisman Club and stared morosely at the neon lights blazing over the nightclub door. He couldn't believe he was facing his first ever blind date. He was going to be forty tomorrow. He wasn't some spotty-faced teenager desperate for a girl. Fenella Grant, sick or not, had an awful

41

lot to answer for. And when she was better, he'd demand it.

He was tempted to drive away and leave Lucinda Burton to her own devices, even if Fenella had claimed the woman was vulnerable. He didn't believe her, not after talking to Lucinda on the phone. But it wasn't in his character to stand a woman up on a date. He sighed. Being a gentleman wasn't always a riot.

The deafening music hit James as soon as he entered the club. It pounded around him and through him, assaulting his eardrums and thumping a beat deep within his chest.

He'd never been to the Talisman before and after a brief scan of the bold flashing lights and gyrating dancers, he knew without a doubt he wouldn't be returning. He preferred something understated and quiet. As he headed for the bar he noticed a woman regarding him in the mirror that ran the full length of the bright red counter. She was noticeable because of her tight-fitting, black sparkly dress and hair that matched the riotous red of the bar.

He hoped the woman wasn't Lucinda. He couldn't be so unlucky.

She smiled. There was nothing vulnerable about her smile. It'd be an appropriate one for a vampire making ready to suck his blood.

He *prayed* she wasn't Lucinda.

The woman smiled wider and wiggled her finger in a coy little wave. The fingernail was tipped in scarlet varnish.

James' heart sank. Was she his prospective date?

'James?' she said over the loud bass beat of the music, her voice low and throbbing with a suggestive bass beat of its own.

His heart sank lower than the floor.

'Lucinda?'

'Glad you could make it, honey.' She held up her glass of red wine and gave him a slow, meaningful once-over. 'Here's to us, party boy. Let's enjoy.'

★　★　★

'Vulnerable! That woman is a man-eater!'

Fen held the phone away from her ear and tried not to giggle.

'Did you hear me?' yelled James.

'Only just. So I gather you had a good evening,' said Fen, unable to keep her chuckle at bay.

'You may well laugh, Ms. Grant. You didn't have to endure it. That Burton woman is a predator. I was lucky to escape in one piece.'

Fen tried to say something soothing but her giggles spilled down the line. They fell on stony silence.

'Are you still there?' she said, hiccoughing and trying to clear her throat. She must compose herself. This was no way to run a business, laughing at the misfortunes of her clients. What was she thinking?

'Yes. Have you quite finished with your ill-timed mirth?'

Another bubble of laughter rose to the surface and escaped before she could stop it. Fen tried to cover it up with a bout of forced coughing. 'Sorry.'

'So you should be.'

'I'll fix you up with someone less . . . strident next time. Just tell me the sort of women you like to date.'

'You must be out of your mind. There will be no next time.'

'But you have a whole year's membership.'

'I don't want it. Give it to someone who's desperate.'

'No, it's all yours. I must apologize about Lucinda. She's in a class of her own. She's a lovely person but she can be a little overpowering. I do have some other women in my files who you may find more to your taste.'

'I'm not having a repeat of last night.'

'It can't have been that bad.'

'Worse.'

Another giggle escaped. Fen clamped her hand over her mouth but she feared she was too late. He was cranky enough without her continuing to laugh at him.

A short, pregnant silence ensued. 'How about I tell you how bad over a drink?' asked James, his voice suddenly soft, as if he was no longer angry, as if he'd forgiven her.

Oops. His suggestion put an abrupt stop to Fen's giggles. James McAllister being nice to her was unexpected. She hadn't been out with anyone since her accident. She might tee up dates for the rest of the world; but for herself, she didn't feel ready to cope.

'I appreciate the invitation, Mr. McAllister,' she said with a no-nonsense coolness. 'But I think it's best if we keep our relationship strictly professional.'

'We don't have a relationship, Ms. Grant,' said James dryly. 'But if you're talking about keeping things business-like, shouldn't you humor your clients and arrange the sort of dates they request?'

'Yes, true, but you just quit your membership, so no can do.'

'But you refused to accept my resignation.'

'I've changed my mind.'

'So have I. I withdraw my resignation

and reinstate myself as a fully paid-up member of Discreet Liaisons.'

'You can't,' she protested.

'I just did.'

'You are the most difficult person I know.' She tried to keep the stroppiness out of her tone.

James laughed. 'Ditto,' he said. 'Which means we should be well suited. A good match. Excellent. Right, when can we meet?'

Never sounded like a good idea! Fen did some rapid thinking. How could she get out of this one? 'It's Sunday. I don't work on Sundays. I'll contact you during the week.' At least that would buy her some time.

'I won't be fobbed off, Ms. Grant.'

'Who said I was fobbing you off?' Her voice rose to a squeak. Fen could have kicked herself.

'Just checking.'

His mildness didn't fool her. He knew she was lying, too. But Fen vowed she'd fob him off if it were the last thing she did. 'Look, I'm sorry, James, but I

47

really must go. I've a hundred and one things to do before the day is through.'

'But — '

'I'll talk to you soon.' Fen hung up quickly and took a deep, steadying breath. Maybe it was time to go and stay at her parents' for a bit of a holiday. Better still, she'd go and see her sister Lynette who was long overdue for a sisterly visit. She would understand why Fen had to hole up for a while and shower her with sisterly sympathy.

3

Fen made it down to her sister's beautiful Sussex flint farmhouse by lunchtime. The Sunday roast was in the oven, vegetables and gravy bubbling on the hob. The sisters sat at the scrubbed pine table and sipped a sherry while they waited for the carrots to cook.

'Well, this is an unexpected pleasure,' said Lynette, clinking Fen's glass with her own and raising her eyebrows in a silent question.

Fen smiled at her sister affectionately, knowing it was only a matter of time before Lynette wheedled out of her the reason for Fen's sudden dash south.

Lynette was five years older than Fen's thirty-one. Her hair was nearer brown than black and much longer than Fen's cropped style. Before the accident, Fen's own hair had been exceptionally long, flowing down to

49

below her waist. When she danced usually she'd swept it into a tight bun. On occasion, though, the character had called for her hair to be loose and it would flow about her lithe frame in lustrous black waves.

But that was once upon a time. The medical staff had shaved it off to deal with her head injuries. Since then Fen had kept it short because it still hurt to raise her arms above her head to wash and brush it. One day she planned to grow it long again.

'I thought it was about time I paid my favorite sister and her gorgeous family a visit,' she said with a bland smile.

Lynette snorted. 'I'm your only sister, though I concede that the rest are gorgeous. But I shan't be deflected. Why are you here? It's not like you to come on an unscheduled visit.'

Unbidden, the image of the darkly attractive James McAllister rose before Fen. As it had been doing all through the night, wickedly teasing her into distracted insomnia. Was there no getting away from him? She sighed, 'I needed a bolt hole for a few days.'

'Because?'

'A client wants to date me rather than my clientele.'

Lynette grinned. 'Sensible man. So why don't you want to go? Does he have two heads and a hunchback?'

'No. One head and no hunchback, though he does have a broken nose.'

'I meant is he ugly?' Lynette wrinkled her nose.

'No. But he's not exactly handsome either.'

'Nasty habits?' Lynette waggled her eyes brows in an all-knowing way.

Fen giggled. 'Not that I know of.'

'So what's the problem?'

'It's against the rules of the agency.'

'You wrote the rules.'

'And I'm hiding behind them,' admitted Fen with rueful honesty.

'Ah hah!' Lynette sounded triumphant.

'And what's 'ah hah' supposed to mean?'

'You like him!'

'Yes, I suppose I do. But I'm not ready for the dating game again.'

'Why ever not?' Lynette rolled her eyes in exasperation. 'You've been doing great since the accident.'

'I still can't walk unaided.'

'But obviously that hasn't put him off so far.'

Fen nibbled her lower lip and gave a small shrug before wrapping her arms defensively around her body. 'Actually, he doesn't know.'

Lynette's jaw dropped. 'But you *have* met him?'

'I was holding on to the door at the time. Most of our conversations have been on the phone.'

'Oh.' Lynette's eyebrows disappeared into her hairline as she regarded her sister with fascinated curiosity. 'So what's the big deal? Just tell him.'

Fen took another sip of sherry and then stared down into the amber liquid, working out how to say what she felt without giving offense.

'Fen?'

'You and the rest of the family and my friends have been great since the accident,' Fen said in a sudden rush. 'But you all treat me so . . . carefully. As though I might break or be hurt or something. He doesn't. He treats me like he would any other person. I don't want to invoke his sympathy or his pity. I want him to treat me as an equal.'

Lynette sucked in a sharp breath. 'I'm sorry if you feel we don't treat you right.'

'I didn't mean to sound ungrateful.' Her sister's tone was defensive, and Fen reached across the table to clasp her sister's hand. 'I've lapped up all the attention.'

'Yes, but Fen, you have to understand, when you had your accident we died a little that day. It hurt us too, you know. We love you.' Her fingers moved to entwine with Fen's.

Fen squeezed affectionately. 'I know and I love you too, sis.'

Lynette sniffed and then blew her

nose on a flimsy bit of tissue she drew from her skirt pocket. 'But how can this man not know about your disability?'

'I don't know. All I do know is that I'm safe from him while I'm here. It'll give me time to figure out what to do next.'

Later that evening, Fen's sister dragged her to her friend's surprise birthday party. She had begged to be allowed to stay at the farmhouse and babysit her niece and nephew.

Lynette pointed out that she'd already booked the teenage babysitter who would be disappointed if she was canceled at the last minute. 'And it'll do you good to socialize, Fen,' she'd declared.

Fen doubted it, but she was no match against her big sister's insistence and she was soon decked out in one of Lynette's dresses, a rich black velvet affair with a medieval-style bodice that dipped low and criss-crossed in front with ribbon lacing. The outfit was set off by a pair of Lynette's flamboyant dangling silver filigree earrings and matching necklace. Though she admitted she looked good, Fen still had to steel herself to enter the Tudor-style manor house where the party was being held.

'I'm not taking my crutches in there,' declared Fen when she saw all the cars parked nose-to-tail in the sweeping driveway. 'I'll damage people's ankles. How about I just sit in the car and listen to the radio.'

'No way,' said Lynette. 'You're not staying out here. You'll freeze to death. You can leave the crutches in the car and just hold on to either Mike or me. We'll steer you to a comfy place where you can sit down and meet loads of interesting people.'

'Can't wait,' muttered Fen. She received a sympathetic glance from her brother-in-law, who had also tried unsuccessfully to avoid the party.

'So whose bash is it?' asked Fen once they had gained the top of the stone steps and peered into the people-packed paneled hallway. Liberal quantities of glossy-leafed, red-berried holly and gold and green streamers festooned the hall's rafters and banisters. A big Christmas tree took pride of place, its pine scent spicing the air. Fen grimaced. Christmas was only a couple of weeks away, and she hadn't yet strung up one bauble or sent a single card. There simply hadn't been the will or the inclination.

'The party's for the brother of my friend Annabelle. Oh, look, there she is over there. Hi, Annabelle!' Lynette was off.

Mike and Fen shared a resigned glance.

'Best get you settled, love,' said Mike. 'Then I'll find us both a nice long drink. We can relax while we blend into the tapestries.'

'You are the very best of brother-in-laws.' Fen kissed him on the cheek.

He found her an alcove window seat where the heavy, gold brocade curtains had been drawn against the bitter night. The room was already overpoweringly warm, and Fen sat there trying to look interested in a potted aspidistra rather than attempt small talk. She really shouldn't have come. She hated this sort of affair.

A little while later, a commotion by the door sounded, followed by a spontaneous singing of happy birthday. The guest of honor had arrived. This was what everyone had been waiting for.

Fen sent up a fervent prayer of thanks. Now she could go home — if only she could pry Lynette away from her partying. Out of curiosity, Fen craned her neck to locate the birthday boy. Through the sea of faces, one man stood out above the rest. Fen froze.

No! It couldn't be! Life couldn't be that cruel.

The man was devastatingly attractive in his dinner jacket. His brown hair was brushed smooth in a slicked-back style to reveal a strong forehead. His shoulders were broad without the aid of coat padding. He smiled with sweet politeness as he accepted birthday greetings from the crowd around him. The women were jostling to kiss him while the men shook his hand.

Fen gulped, panic causing a hard lump in her throat which threatened to shut off her air supply. What rotten luck. This must be a bad dream. Or a *Candid Camera* set-up. Or maybe she was hallucinating. What had been in that yummy mushroom quiche she'd eaten at lunch? Whatever the reason, Fen felt the best course of action was to hide behind the brocade drapes before he spotted her.

'Why are you skulking here?' demanded Lynette a few minutes later. 'I know you don't like these sorts of affairs, but playing hide-and-seek behind the curtains is weird, even for you.'

'This is the best place for me. I can people-watch to my heart's content.' Especially one person whom she didn't want to encounter in a pink fit.

'But you're not mixing.'

'I'm blending, though. There's a subtle but significant difference.'

'The only blending you're doing is with the curtain.'

'You're wrong. You just haven't seen me when I've been chatting.' She batted her eyelashes. Then, to keep Lynette happy, she added, 'So fill me in on who is here. What's the gossip?'

Lynette took the bait and sat down next to her to tell her about a load of local people Fen would probably never meet again. Finally Lynette got around to mentioning Annabelle's brother whom Fen did — but didn't — want to know about.

'So what's his story?' Fen fished. Her eyes downcast, she pleated the velvet folds of her skirt over and over again with fingers that trembled slightly, much to her annoyance. But she affected a neutral tone. No way did she want to alert Lynette to the depth of her interest in James. Yes, so her curiosity was aroused, but Lynette didn't need to be privy to that.

'Forty, single, successful and attractive. Annabelle is always complaining about his Gorgeous Gazelles, so I told her about your agency.'

'Gorgeous Gazelles?' That little gem hadn't appeared on his résumé his sister gave her.

'He serial dates models. They're tall, slim and flighty. Did she contact you?'

'Belle McAllister,' said Fen in a flat monotone.

'I'm sorry?'

'You, dear sister, didn't tell me Annabelle Saunders was Belle McAllister.' Doomsday for Fen. She'd marched smack into danger and only some pretty fast-talking would get her marched straight out of it.

'McAllister is Annabelle's maiden name. Is it relevant?'

'To me, yes. Annabelle bought a membership for her brother's birthday present last week.'

'And?'

Fen groaned and dropped her head in her hands. 'James McAllister is the man I'm trying to avoid,' she said, her voice muffled by the tightness in her throat.

'Oh Lord.'

'And I want to go home. Now!' She lifted her head and stared hard at Lynette. 'And no quibbling, sister.'

* * *

When he saw the crowded party, James' heart sank. Annabelle had excelled herself. She'd pulled out all the stops, along with extra bells and whistles. So much for the small celebration to mark his fortieth. Obviously her idea of small and his were poles apart.

The party was in full swing. He greeted old friends and acquaintances and wished he were a hundred miles away. Better still, he wished he were having an intimate drink with the engaging Ms. Grant in some dimly lit, secluded bar where it was just the two of them. But the experience would have to remain on hold for the foreseeable future, mainly because of the reluctance of Ms. Grant to go out with him, but also because he couldn't disappoint Annabelle. She'd gone to so much effort to stage this party, so he'd better make the best of the evening ahead.

James squared his shoulders and curved his lips into a determined smile. Time to do the party circuit. He strode with purposeful *bonhomie* into the room and, with gracious regard for his sister's reputation, was polite to everyone. Several minutes into his ordeal James felt a prickle at the back of his neck, as if he was being watched with the intensity of a laser beam. He did a quick scan of faces before being monopolized by a beautiful, tall blonde whom he'd dated on a couple of occasions during the summer.

The woman failed to hold his complete attention and James let his gaze wander back around the room. It skimmed over a slight young woman in a black dress who was in earnest conversation with another woman whom James recognized as one of

Annabelle's close friends from the village. His gaze moved on, only to bounce back a split second later.

The crazy cropped hair. Pale skin. The incredible fine bone structure and air of fragility. He'd know her anywhere. His heart pounded an excited beat, thumping against his ribcage and causing his pulse to echo the rhythm. Now, suddenly, the evening was on a definite upward swing. *Thank you, Belle.*

'Excuse me,' said James, cutting the blonde off in mid-sentence. 'I've just seen someone I must talk to.'

He elbowed his way through the chattering couples and zeroed in on the two women in the alcove who were preparing to leave. They were both standing and Fenella Grant had her hand on the other woman's arm. He was just in time to stop them.

'Ms. Grant,' he said. 'What a fantastic surprise. But tell me you're not going already? I've only just arrived.'

'Oh God, that's torn it,' said Fen,

plopping back in her seat.

James was taken aback at her tragic expression. 'Anything wrong?' he ventured, his voice wary.

'No, just Fen overreacting as per usual,' said the other woman with a bubbly laugh. 'I'm Lynette, Fen's sister. You probably don't remember me, but we met at Belle's last party in July.'

'Yes, of course I remember. We all got drenched in a sudden summer storm.' It was the same party where he'd met the blonde.

'So a very happy birthday is in order.' Lynette kissed his cheek. 'Congratulations on surviving forty years.' She gave another of her contagious laughs.

James smiled, but he wished Fen had dished out the kisses. When he'd glanced at her, she was looking like a trapped wild cat that would bolt at the first opportunity. Kissing him appeared to be the last thing on her mind. 'Clever me,' he said. 'But I have been assured that forty isn't over the hill. And lots of women find the more, er, mature man irresistible.'

'My husband would agree with you there,' said Lynette. 'And talking of Mike, I must go and find him and make sure he's behaving himself. Do excuse me.' Lynette squeezed Fen's shoulder. 'I'll be back in a minute, Fen.'

After Lynette's departure, James made his move. 'Do I get a birthday kiss from you too?' he asked Fen with a smile.

'Maybe. I'll think about it.' She avoided his eyes and resumed her nervous pleating of her skirt.

'You're looking beautiful tonight.' He sat next to Fen, his knee grazing the rich velvet material.

'Actually, I think the pajamas have the edge.'

She twitched her skirt away from his leg as if she was avoiding all contact.

James, a tactile person himself, found her standoffishness amusing. 'And the earrings are exquisite.' He fingered one of the delicate pieces of jewelry and felt Fen tremble. He had to admit, he felt a

65

few trembles himself. His body reacted to hers in a primeval, sexy way which he found intriguing, as well as surprising.

She wasn't his usual type, but there was something about Fenella Grant that attracted him deep down. He suddenly had the incredible urge to lean forward and place his lips on the pulse he could see flickering at the base of her slender throat. To kiss her and see how she would respond. Instead, he wrenched his concentration back to what Fen was saying.

They're my sister's, as is the dress. I wasn't expecting to attend a party tonight. I'd only packed jeans, a sweater and woolly socks.'

'Oh, so you're not here for my benefit?' Disappointment rippled through him.

'No. If I'd known it was your birthday we were celebrating, I would have pleaded the plague. I'm not meant to meet my clients socially. It says so in — '

'The agency rule book. I remember. But I'd hoped you were relaxing them for me or had at least decided to be my date for the night.'

Fen rolled her eyes. 'I treat all my clients the same. No playing favorites.'

'You're a hard woman.' James shook his head in exasperation.

'I like to think so.'

'So how come a tough, professional woman such as yourself has become involved in the love game?'

He watched Fen's cheeks go pink. 'It's more of a friendship agency than anything else,' she said quickly. 'I set it up for companionship rather than love affairs. It's all aboveboard. There's nothing tacky.'

'I wasn't inferring it was. Have any of your couples fallen in love and tied the knot?'

'The agency hasn't been going that long,' she said with a lofty tilt of her chin.

'How long?' He watched with amusement as she hesitated, perhaps wondering whether or not to tell him.

She sighed and slumped against the cushions in defeat. 'Two months,' she admitted.

James was surprised. 'Is that all? So what were you doing before that?'

Her brows quirked in a suspicious frown. 'Why do you want to know?'

'Because I'm curious.'

'Why?' she persisted.

'Why don't you want to tell me? What are you hiding?' It was his turn to frown.

'I'm not.' She crossed her arms over her chest and glared at him, defying him to continue.

'So why not say? Were you a top-level spy or something equally secretive?' He attempted to lighten the atmosphere, which was in danger of becoming arctic.

'Don't be ridiculous.'

'So tell me, Fen,' he implored.

'No. It's private. I don't discuss my private life with my clients.'

'I resign,' he declared with promptness and grinned.

'Again? Why?'

Her whole demeanor was still suspicious, which made James more determined to discover what she was hiding. 'So we can start again, this time as friends rather than business associates.'

'I'm still not going to tell you so you might as well give up now.'

'Okay, let's dance instead.' James was surprised to see an emotion akin to panic flare in her deep blue eyes.

'No! I . . . er . . . still don't feel well enough to fandango around a dance floor.'

'I'll request a smoochy number. I'm not into . . . er . . . fandangoing, whatever it may be.'

'I don't want to dance. In fact, we're leaving in a minute.'

'But the night is young. The party's only just beginning to crank up.'

'I have to go. I have to work tomorrow.'

James scowled. He disliked being blocked from his goal and he wasn't used to resistance from a woman. But he wouldn't give up, however hard she tried to cold shoulder him. 'How are you getting back to London? Would you like me to drive you?'

'No!'

There was the panic again. James found it disconcerting. 'Is it just me or are you usually this cagey?'

'She's always this cagey. It's her nature,' said Lynette, interrupting them with an apologetic smile. 'I'm sorry, James, but we have to get back home for the babysitter. It's been a great party. Thank you.'

'How about I drop Fen off later?' He knew he was clutching at straws. One look at Fen's aghast face told him he was doomed to be disappointed. She didn't even try to hide her dismay, which wasn't very flattering for his ego.

'I appreciate the offer,' said Fen, casting a swift, anxious glance at her sister that made James even more puzzled. 'But I need an early night as I am still recuperating from my . . . illness.'

James immediately felt contrite. How could he have forgotten she'd been ill? 'Of course, I'm sorry. I'll ring you during the week to discuss our drink.' He leaned forward and kissed her cheek. Her skin was smooth and warm under his lips, just as he'd imagined it would be. He would have liked to linger there for a precious moment, inhaling her delicate flowery fragrance, but the others were hovering ready to leave.

Mike held out his arm to Fen and she hauled herself to her feet while Lynette distracted James by brushing some imaginary lint off his dinner jacket. Lynette then moved to Fen's other side and threaded her arm around her little sister's waist.

James wished he was clasping Fen's narrow waist, but it would have been rude to have muscled in on Lynette. He had to be content to simply walk them to the door. Progress was slow as many goodbyes were said on the way, but that didn't worry James. He was happy to watch Fen and her gentle smile and wish that she'd bestow some of her sweetness on him.

'Don't come out in the cold, James,' said Fen as she stood on the stone steps for the second time that night. 'Go back in and enjoy the rest of your party.'

'What about my birthday kiss?' James couldn't resist. He had to kiss her again. Feel her satin skin under his lips. 'Don't I deserve one?'

'Well, I — '

'Excuse me.' James stepped forward and with consummate skill blocked out Mike and Lynette. They were forced to drop away from flanking Fen so she was open and vulnerable to his onslaught.

James wasted no time sliding his arm around Fen's waist and sweeping her close to his chest. His mouth swooped down over hers and he felt her soft lips melt and move under his. The kiss was swift and sure. If there hadn't been an audience, he would have continued experiencing the sweet paradise of her mouth. But they weren't alone and he had to behave himself or he'd embarrass all four of them.

James pulled back. His eyes met Fen's and for a breathless instant he was sure he read a deep longing in their midnight blue depths which he knew was reflected in his. He moved to kiss her again, but his sister Annabelle broke the tenuous spell.

'James! James!' she called. 'Time to cut the cake.'

Fen blinked. Her eyes refocused.

James knew she was grappling to re-erect the shutters over those expressive windows of her heart. He offered her a small, and what he hoped was appealing, smile, not wanting to let her go. 'Can I tempt you to a piece of birthday cake, Fen? It's guaranteed to be rich and chocolaty with loads of cream, if Annabelle has had anything to do with it.'

'It sounds delicious, but no. Sorry.' Her voice sounded a hundred miles away. 'We do have to go. Babysitters and all that.'

'James, now!' called Annabelle from inside. 'Or the candles will melt the chocolate!'

'I'll be in touch,' said James, and with regretful reluctance he released her to attend to his birthday duties.

4

'Phew. That was a close call,' said Lynette as they scrunched across the frosty, snow-covered gravel towards their Range Rover.

'You're telling me,' muttered Fen, shivering under her wrap and wishing she'd never set foot inside the party. It was exactly the kind of event that left her feeling inadequate, in spite of James' explosive kiss which was still sending Richter scale shock waves through her body.

Her feelings of inadequacy were compounded after witnessing James chatting with a beautiful blonde who was no doubt one of his so-called Gorgeous Gazelles. The woman had only emphasized Fen's lack of inches and crippled legs. James may not realize it, but he instinctively sought physical perfection in his women. He might be intrigued by Fen for some bizarre reason, but his interest wouldn't last. Of that she was sure.

'And that was some goodbye kiss,' carried on Lynette, huffing on her fingers and stamping her feet as she waited for Mike to unlock the car.

'It was,' agreed Fen. Well, what else could she say? It had been. There was no denying it. Surprisingly, the snow hadn't melted in the fallout. 'Lucky me.'

'I never got our drinks,' said Mike, tucking Fen into the back seat. 'That must be the fastest party on record. Can you hang around for the rest of the Christmas season, Fen, and put the jinx on all the other village socials?'

His wife gave him a playful punch on the arm. 'Don't be such a kill joy. Parties are fun.'

'So why did we leave early?' asked Mike. 'Will someone please explain?'

Lynette and Fen exchanged a knowing look. 'No,' they said in unison, and then they both laughed at his puzzled expression.

The next morning, a silver Jensen drove into the farm's central courtyard and parked outside the house.

'Who do we know with a silver car?' asked Lynette, squinting out the kitchen window, her view obscured by flurries of snowflakes.

'Oh no! It's James!' Fen gave a tiny shriek. 'And I'm still in my PJs.' They were Winnie the Pooh ones this time. Perhaps she ought to think about upgrading if he was going to make a habit of early morning visits.

'Quick. Go and get changed.'

'Dear sister, quick is not in my vocabulary these days.'

'Sorry. I forgot. There's no time anyway. He's right by the door.' Lynette swung it open before James knocked. 'Morning, James. Come in.'

Come in? Come in? Where was sisterly solidarity when you needed it? Fen glared at Lynette and then glared at James for good measure. He looked like Harrison Ford in his black wool overcoat sprinkled with snow. Flakes were melting into his hair and those bags were back again. He must have gone to bed late. She thought crankily how James must have been enjoying the company of the luscious blonde during the evening's frivolity.

James gave her a slightly crooked smile, as if unsure of his welcome. So he should be, she decided. He presumed too much, both last night with his spine-tingling kiss and this morning, arriving unannounced and hung-over, if his weary expression was anything to go by.

'You look tired. Good night, I suppose?' said Fen with a caustic edge to her voice and not employing an ounce of tact.

'Very.' He strode further into the kitchen and, much to Fen's surprise, dropped a kiss on her spiky, uncombed bed-hair. 'Like the pajamas.' He fingered her sleeve. 'But I prefer the Garfield ones.'

'Have you time for a cuppa?' asked Lynette, whose eyebrows were hitting her hairline at the pajama crack.

Fen, with a sinking heart, knew detailed explanations would be demanded as soon as James was out of the door.

'Please,' said James.

'Don't you have to drive to the city?' Fen asked with a bluntness that bordered on rude. But she didn't care. The quicker James left the more relaxed she would feel.

'Yes. I came to see if you'd changed your mind and wanted a lift.'

'I have changed my mind. I'm not going to London at all. I'm staying here for a few days to help Lyn with the Christmas baking.'

'You are?' said Lynette, her mouth forming a complete round of surprise and her eyes blinking rapidly.

'I am,' she replied firmly.

'That's a shame. I could have done with the company.' His lips quirked in a regretful manner.

Fen was far too conscious of his hang-dog expression, which was no doubt to appeal to her better nature and make her change her mind. Hah. It didn't work. She was made of sterner stuff. 'I've got my laptop with me. I might be able to find you a suitable candidate from my files who can fill the breach.'

'Forget I said anything,' said James, holding up his hands in a defensive pose. 'I couldn't bear another run-in with a Lucinda-type. Suddenly solitary driving sounds great.'

'You are so chicken.'

James dropped his hands and stuck them on his hips. 'And you, my sweet, are a coward. Why don't you want to spend time with me?' He held her eyes with his steady gaze, challenging her.

Fen tried not to squirm like a speared worm on the end of a fish hook, but it was hard remaining aloof. 'I don't mind spending time with you,' she hedged.

'Good. Progress at last. So about this drink you promised me?'

'Soon.' She was back to squirming.

'Coward.'

She responded to the jibe, which was probably what he intended. 'Okay, Wednesday.'

'Done.' And he grinned at her as Lynette handed him his mug of tea. 'Now,' he said. 'That wasn't so hard, was it, Ms. Grant?'

Fen gave him a hard stare and he laughed out loud, but didn't push the point further. He was content to drink his tea and chat to Lynette about village life, tossing the occasional warm glance in Fen's direction. Those glances weren't lost on either sister. One found them amusing, the other wanted to crawl under the table and die of embarrassment.

'So,' said Lynette after James had left. 'How are you going to weasel out of your little date?'

'I'll think of something.' Fen nibbled the top of her finger and thought of a hundred ways to get out of seeing James, but rejected them in the next instance. Trips to Outer Mongolia and flying to the moon were not logical.

'Just come clean, why don't you?' suggested her sister.

Fen rolled her eyes in disgust.

'Not an option,' said Fen. 'I do not want him to know I'm crippled. While I think of a plan, I'd better get dressed before we have any other visitors. Then I must make some mince pies to earn my keep.'

Wednesday came around too fast, but Fen had everything planned and ready to roll. She was meeting James at a small bar not far from her home. She'd get there early, hide her crutches under the bench and then stay glued to the seat until The Phone Call.

The phone call would be for James. She'd organized with Belle, via Lynette, for Belle to ring his mobile and make up some excuse for him to leave the bar. He'd go, Fen would retrieve her crutches, hop into a taxi and James would be none the wiser about her wonky legs. Brilliant.

Brilliant, except it was the pre-Christmas silly season and the bar was packed. Brilliant, except it took Fen so long to find a seat she'd only just stowed her crutches under the bench before James arrived, which meant she was all hot and bothered. And brilliant, except James was far, far too early by a good fifteen minutes, and she hadn't enough time to center herself. Instead, she was flushed and flustered. He probably thought that was because of him, which irked her no end.

'You're early,' she accused while surreptitiously using her heel to push the crutches further under the bench and out of sight.

'So are you. You must have been as anxious to see me as I was to see you.' He bent over and kissed the tip of her nose, then grinned.

His action threw Fen. No one kissed her on the nose. It was too bold, too familiar.

'I thought we'd have a drink here and then go on somewhere for dinner,' said James. 'I ordered us a bottle of Merlot. We can drink the wine while we decide where we should eat. There are several good places around here. I recommend the Thai round the corner.'

Fen's plans were unraveling at the speed of light and she tried not to panic. 'But you said we were meeting for just a drink.' The Thai and any other restaurant were not to be considered.

'Live dangerously, darling.'

'This is dangerous enough for me, thank you,' said Fen with repressive force.

James chuckled and clinked her wine glass with his. 'Here's to us and living dangerously.'

His tone was low and warm and sexy. Fen's heart skipped a couple of beats, or six. She didn't know if it was safe to drink to his toast. She wasn't sure what he wanted of her and was equally unsure what she wanted of him. Though, to be realistic, she should ask for nothing at this point of her life. The thought shafted her heart with breathtaking speed and caught her on the raw. 'Nothing' was too tragic to contemplate.

She thrust the negative thought away. She must concentrate on the here and now and getting away from James unscathed both in heart and mind. 'Cheers,' she mumbled, feeling it would be for the best if the evening finished before it actually started. She willed Belle to ring, reciting the mantra in her brain: *please ring, please ring, please ring* . . .

On cue, James' mobile rang.

Yes!

'Curse the thing,' he said and switched it off.

Fen opened and shut her mouth a couple of times in mute alarm. 'Shouldn't you answer it?' They'd be stuck here all night if he didn't answer the wretched phone. Bother, she should have had a Plan B tucked away for such an emergency as this.

James shrugged. 'If it's important, they'll leave a message.'

Fen took a hefty gulp of wine while she regrouped. Now what? 'You'd best have a look to see if they have,' she insisted.

'Relax, Fen.'

Relax? Relax! How could she? Her secret could be discovered any moment and then where would they be? He'd end up feeling sorry for her and showering her with pity and she'd lose her hard-fought desire to be treated as an able-bodied date!

Date. Did she really mean date? They were just sharing a drink. It wasn't really a proper date. And would it really, really matter if he discovered her infirmity?

Yes! It mattered. This might not be a romantic date but there was a certain amount of swirling vibes going on and she didn't want to spoil things. At least not yet. She'd have to think of a diversion. She scanned the noisy bar.

People chatted and laughed. Glasses clinked. Music throbbed in a muted beat in the background. None of it inspired her. Try as she might, she couldn't think how she could escape

James without giving the game away.

They were almost to the end of the bottle when they were interrupted by a member of the bar staff. 'Mr. McAllister, there's a call for you.'

Fen almost cheered out loud, feeling a great swell of relief in her churned-up tummy, as James followed the staff member to the bar. Belle must have found out from Lynette where she and James were having their drink. Phew. She wondered what excuse Belle had concocted that would make James leave in a hurry? She didn't have long to wait.

He strode back to their table, his face a set mask. 'I'm dreadfully sorry, Fen, but we've got to go.'

We? No, that wasn't in the equation. *He* had to go!

'What's happened?' Fen watched him gather up their coats. He held out his hand to assist her to stand. Fen clutched the edge of her seat, her fingernails burying into the upholstery, and tried not to panic.

'My house is on fire,' he said with amazing calm.

Fen inwardly groaned. Excellent one, Belle! Talk about spinning a yarn that was completely over the top. But Fen was suitably impressed by James' lack of emotion. If it had been her house going up in smoke, she would have been ranting and raving and yelling 'fire' at the top of her voice.

'Oh no! How dreadful. You'd better hurry. Don't worry about me. I can easily find my way home.' Was that too glib? She hoped not. But if he was being so laid-back about the alleged fire, why couldn't she?

'I can't leave you here alone.'

'Sure you can. I came under my own steam and I'm happy to leave the same way.' *Bet your bottom dollar, McAllister!*

'But that's not the way I do things.' He continued to hold out his hand.

Fen gripped the seat edge harder, almost taking out chunks of the furry fabric, and swallowed nervously. 'Your house fire is far more important than getting me home, really. Go. Go now.' *Please!*

'Fen!'

'I won't hold it against you. Honest.'

He hesitated. His brow creased and his mouth was a grim line. 'Okay. I'll ring you.' He leaned over and kissed her hard and briefly on the lips.

His kiss made them tingle. It made her toes tingle. It was power-packed.

'Bye,' he said.

And Fen just mouthed a farewell because her vocal cords had momentarily seized up with the intensity of his embrace.

As soon as he'd gone, Fen hauled out her mobile phone from her coat pocket and rang for a taxi. She then retrieved her crutches. She was safe from James' probing for a while longer at least, but she wasn't going to hang around, just in case. A quick visit to the restroom and she'd be gone.

As she returned to the smoky bar, she saw James. Eek! He stood by their table, which was already occupied by another couple, and scanning the haze-filled room, looking for her. Fen ducked back into the ladies room and stayed there for what seemed like forever.

She then made a hurried exit from the bar and found her waiting taxi.

A while later, James called her at the flat. 'There was no fire,' he said.

His voice was calm and measured, and ... suspicious. Or was that just Fen's guilty conscience fanning her imagination? Fen squirmed and twisted the telephone cord around her finger. 'Thank goodness. What a relief.'

'I rang the fire department while waiting for the taxi. They knew nothing about it.'

'Gosh.' Good grief, she hadn't expected him to ring the fire brigade. What sort of man did that? A suspicious one, that's who.

'So I cancelled the taxi and went back into the bar.'

'Oh.' Fen had a hot flash from top to

toe. James was one swift worker. She hadn't even supposed he'd be back in the bar so fast.

'You'd already gone.'

'Ah.' Fen tried to sound apologetic, but golly, they must have missed each other by seconds. Split seconds, even. She squeezed shut her eyes and did a rapid prayer of thanks.

'That was quick. Would you like to explain?' James still sounded reasonable. Maybe it was only Fen's guilty conscience that was seeking suspicion in his every nuance.

'Yes. I . . . er . . . didn't think you'd be back.' She tried not to gabble.

'Fen, I was gone less than five minutes.'

Grief, yes, it had been a close call. Good job she hadn't tarried. 'Oh,' she said with pathetic lameness.

'So?' said James. A pregnant pause, the size of a small country, swelled up between them.

'So?' echoed Fen eventually, wondering what was coming next.

'I suppose it's a bit late for me to come around and finish off our evening.'

Was he asking her or telling her? She couldn't tell from the timbre of his voice. 'It is a bit,' said Fen, biting her lip and wishing things could be different between them.

'Shame.' Real regret colored the word.

'Yes. But good news about the fire. Or lack of it.'

A heart's beat pause throbbed. 'Good night, Fenella Grant.'

He suspected she was behind the false fire call. Fen was sure of it. Oh well, it had been a risk. At least she lived to fight another day.

And she had enjoyed their drink together, very, very much, in spite of the stress of keeping her secret.

★   ★   ★

'Do you want to go shopping, Fen?' Fen's West Indian neighbor Trish asked

92

two days later, after Fen had returned from her sister's. 'Christmas will soon be upon us, babe, and I'm beginning to panic. I've got no stocking fillers for my sweet boys.'

As Trish's 'sweet boys' were typical teenagers into rap and football and hanging around on street corners, Fen was amused they still had stockings from Santa. But then who was she to laugh? Her mum still gave her a stocking stuffed full of goodies on Christmas morning, too.

'Sounds good to me,' said Fen, shutting down her computer; she'd been lining up some pre-Christmas dates for clients. Unfortunately, James McAllister hadn't been among them. He'd been her only client who hadn't been clamoring for dates. He hadn't even called her. She didn't know whether to feel disappointed or relieved.

'There's one condition though,' Trish went on. 'I want you to go in your wheelchair.'

'But Trish! No way.' Fen hated the

wheelchair with a passion. It reminded her of all the months of misery and pain in hospital.

'Hear me out, girl. Since the kiddies have grown up, I've really missed the convenience of piling my shopping on a pushchair. Your wheelchair is second best. You got a problem with that?'

'Yes. Buy one of those shopping bags on wheels.'

'What? A roll-around cart! They're for old people.'

'And you don't qualify?' joked Fen.

'You're wicked,' said Trish. 'I might be widowed and have two high school kids, but there's still plenty of life left in me, which is why I joined your matchmaking agency. If you don't indulge one of your most valued clients, babe, I'm withdrawing my membership.'

Where had Fen heard that one before? In her opinion, her clients were getting much too demanding for comfort. Which was why she should tighten the rules and not sign up friends or get too personal with clients, like James.

Trish good-naturedly hassled her some more, so Fen reluctantly conceded to her request and had to put up with the ignobility of being pushed around the dozens of market stalls set up in the Portobello Road. Actually, riding was easier and less tiring than trying to maneuver with her crutches, but Fen wouldn't admit it, even to herself.

A couple of hours later, while they were having a hilarious time trying on some garish hats, Fen almost keeled over on the spot when she saw James. Good grief. What on earth was he doing in Portobello Road? The man worked in the city. So why was he in her locality?

Paying no attention to the thronging street market, James strode the pavement in the direction of her home, dodging shoppers and dawdlers alike, as though he was a man on a mission. In one hand he held a brown leather briefcase, in the other a big bunch of dusky pink, shaggy-headed chrysanthemums. And he was getting much too close to where Fen was stuck in her wheelchair. Any moment now and he'd see her.

'Eek,' she squeaked and grabbed a hideous purple hat from the stand. She rammed it on her head, pulling it low over her eyes.

'Doesn't suit you, babe,' said Trish, who whisked off the offending hat and popped a lime green one on in its place. She stepped back a pace, thrust her hands on her hips and cocked her head to one side. 'No, still not you.'

Fen snatched at the green hat before Trish could take it off too and held it close to her scalp, shielding her face as much as possible with the wide floppy brim.

'Hey, girl, what's got into you? Lime green is so not you. Try orange.'

Fen ignored her and slunk down low in her wheelchair. 'Leave me be.'

'You having a turn or something, or just being plain awkward?' asked Trish.

'I don't want to be seen,' muttered Fen.

'Babe, wearing a bright green hat is not what I'd call camouflage.' Trish gave a shout of laughter and slapped her ample thigh.

'It's better than nothing.' Fen peeked out from under the felt brim and spotted James' back view several stalls away. Phew. That had been close. She wrenched off the hat and flung it on the pile of others.

'Hey, lady,' said the stall owner. 'You gonna buy that hat after manhandling it, or what?'

'Sorry?' She struggled to concentrate on the man but it wasn't easy. Her blood was pumping hard from the sudden surge of adrenalin caused by seeing James. She was almost light-headed with relief that he'd gone without spotting her.

'The hat, lady. You want it?'

'No.'

'But you've stretched the brim. It's ruined.'

'Oh, come on,' spluttered Fen.

'Make it half price and she will,' said Trish, who always enjoyed a good haggle.

'Daylight robbery. How about a fiver?'

'Done! Pay the man, Fen, and then let's head home. I could murder a coffee,' said Trish, trying on the hat herself and preening in front of the mirror.

'Home is not an option,' stated Fen, who had no intention of going any-where near her flat in case James was lurking there. She dug out a five-pound note for the man and handed it over. 'Let's find the nearest café, Trish. My treat.'

'If you've got money to burn, girl, that's fine by me. But I demand to know why you're suddenly into all the cloak-and-dagger stuff. I smell a good mystery.'

5

James rang the doorbell and knocked several times. Obviously Fen wasn't home. Frustration gnawed deep down. He stared morosely at the pink chrysanthemums. Why did it matter whether or not he saw her? She wasn't exactly falling over herself to spend time with him. Perhaps he should take the hint.

But, no. He was sure she was as attracted to him as he was to her. He felt it in the air. A special crackle between them when thet were together. He saw it shimmering in her gorgeous blue eyes. He felt it deep in his heart . . .

Mind, he'd been certain she'd been behind the crank fire call. But why? What was the point? She only had to say she didn't want to go out with him. He wouldn't force her. But he wondered if that was the case. He sensed she was more interested in him than she cared to admit, to him and maybe herself. Or perhaps she simply liked playing psychological games? It raised the stakes, made the dating game more interesting.

But there again, he didn't *think* she was a nutter, not like those women he'd passed in the market trying on outrageous hats, even if she did have a penchant for cartoon pajamas . . .

Dropping the chrysanthemums on the doorstep, James decided to call Annabelle. He'd get her to ring Lynette and ask her if she had any idea where Fen would be on a Friday afternoon. While he waited for her to ring back, James looked for a café to have a coffee.

Plenty of cafés along the Portobello Road. James randomly chose one, gave his order to the young waitress and then settled himself at a window table to read the *Financial Times* newspaper.

As he received his coffee, he saw a rather large West Indian lady on the street side of the café's plate glass window. She gave him a blatant once over and then an audacious wink as she headed off down the pavement, pushing a person in a wheelchair who was wearing a revolting green hat.

Before he could wonder just what the woman was winking at, his phone rang. Annabelle was returning his call and she had the information he'd requested. James grinned as he terminated the call and he scribbled down the name of a nearby gym. So Fen worked out, did she? Good girl. His grin widened as he imagined Fen in body-hugging Lycra. Boy, he could hardly wait.

And wouldn't she be surprised to see him.

★ ★ ★

Fen had experienced far too much excitement for one day. Seeing James in the market had been one thing. Having him come into the same café had been more than a tad uncomfortable. She'd broken out in an instant cold sweat and had scalded her tongue on a big gulp of cappuccino to compensate.

And now here were the flowers, lying forlornly on her doorstep. Some of the dusky pink petals had been blown by the wind and were scattered like confetti on the pavement. Fen sucked on her bottom lip. Why was James visiting her flat — and did he intend to come back later?

Did she want him to?

Her heart skittered a spasm and she closed her eyes. Yes. No. Maybe. Well, perhaps it was a blessing that she wouldn't be here if he did. Her appointment at the gym, to go through her thrice-weekly workout with her fitness instructor and friend Gail, was most important. If she missed the workout, she would lose ground on her fitness regime, and she didn't want to do that, especially now. Having James McAllister in the equation gave her a huge incentive boost to toss away her crutches and get walking.

Sometime later Fen was flat on her

back and ten minutes into her floor exercises when she heard the woman next to her say, 'Wow, now that's what I call a good body.'

Fen raised her head and glanced in the same direction as her fellow exerciser and instantly experienced another burst of cold sweat.

James.

There was no disputing the good body tag. He looked gorgeous in his silky black shorts and white T-shirt. His legs were muscular, as were his arms. By the way he filled out his T-shirt, his chest had the full quota of muscles too. Darn it, the man was just too attractive for comfort. Avoiding him was such a tragedy. But it had to be done, right? At least for the next few weeks, or months — but pray not years — until she could walk again. Then James McAllister, watch out!

Fen sighed and flopped back on the mat. What wicked fate had brought James to her gymnasium? And on a Friday afternoon, too? What was wrong with the man? Didn't he have a job to go to? A multi-million-dollar business to run?

'This calls for a few more tummy tightening exercises to tone me up,' said Fen's companion with a grin. 'And then I'm going to claim that exercise bike right next to his. Wish me luck.'

'You've got it.'

Fen lay still on the mat, madly trying to work out how she could get to the changing rooms without using her crutches. If she could just reach out, she might be able to push them under the nearby rowing machine.

She stretched. Rats, she was short by a foot. She could have reached them if she could have used her legs. But then, if she could have used her legs, she wouldn't need the crutches and so wouldn't be in this pickle.

There was only one thing for it. She would have to roll over to reach them. She spun over a couple of times and then tucked the crutches out of sight. Hopefully, nobody wanted to use the machine in the next few minutes.

She then rolled back on to her mat and wondered what to do next. She lifted her head to take another peek at James. The woman in her skin-tight, sky-blue Lycra was leaning on James' handlebars and granting him a great eyeful of her voluptuous figure. The woman had no shame, thought Fen, but at least she was keeping James occupied. If she monopolized him long enough, Fen might be able to crawl or roll or do whatever to reach the changing rooms. Better still, lie here flat and hope James would eventually go away.

Yes, that was the best option. At least until she could think of a better plan. She rotated her feet, stretched out her toes and stared at the ceiling, imagining her worst-case scenario. James would see her and come over while she was lying like a stranded beetle, arms and legs flailing in the air.

Fate couldn't be so cruel. It wouldn't happen. It was just a fluke James was here. He didn't know she belonged to this gym. How could he? She hadn't told him. So just think positive and get on with the exercises.

'Are you in pain, Fen?' Gail asked, looking efficient and fit in her navy and white instructor's uniform and her blonde-streaked hair tied back in a jaunty ponytail. She strode over to where Fen was trying to sink into the floor and look as though she was part of the gymnasium carpet.

'No more than usual,' said Fen. 'Have you come to bully me into doing extra?'

'Yes. You looked as though you were slacking off. Or are those rolls a new variation to your routine that I don't know about?'

Fen offered her a twisted smile. 'I was getting my crutches out of the way.'

'Any particular reason?'

'Yes. Him.' Fen nodded in the direction of James. No point being coy. Fen would have to enlist Gail's help to scuttle back to the changing rooms.

'Oh, I see. Well, he's certainly creating a bit of a stir.' She glanced around the room. 'The ladies are all trying very hard to look taut and terrific. But I'm surprised you've fallen under his spell. I didn't think you were on a manhunt. You've been adamant about no dates since the accident.'

'I'm not on a manhunt or under his spell,' Fen spluttered with self-righteous indignation. 'I just don't want him to know I'm a cripple.'

Gail snorted. 'You aren't a cripple. You're simply injured. It won't be long before you're back on your feet again.'

'Yes, but I do need crutches at the moment and I don't want James to realize that.'

'So, it's James, is it?'

Darn, Fen had let his name slip out. If she wasn't careful, Gail would want the third degree and she didn't feel like obliging. The less she said about James the better. 'He's just a . . . friend,' she muttered.

'Ah.'

The 'ah' held far too much significance for Fen's comfort. Gail was no fool. 'An acquaintance,' she added. It was hard to look lofty while lying flat on one's back and doing six-inch leg raises, but Fen tried anyway.

'I see.' Gail giggled. 'Thousands wouldn't, but I believe you.'

Fen flopped her leg down and huffed her defeat. 'Well, actually he's one of my clients.'

'Oh, right. A client. So how come you've never fixed me up with him?'

Gail had been one of Fen's first Discreet Liaisons' sign ups and had used the agency on several occasions. Now it was Fen's turn to laugh. 'Because he's new on the books and has only had one date.'

'With you?' Gail accused with mock seriousness.

'No, not with me.' Fen decided not to tell her about their drink and fire drill. Too complicated. 'I don't date my clients.'

'But he could be an exception, right?'

Gail glanced over to where James was still pedaling at breakneck speed on the exercise bike. 'Personally I would break ALL the rules to date him.'

'Okay, so I'm tempted. I'm only human. But I'm not going to even try and get him interested until I can walk again. I don't want him feeling sorry for me.' Fen made another half-hearted leg raise, four inches this time, winced, and then relaxed her leg.

'Hence hiding the crutches.'

'Yes. And if you get me into the changing rooms without James spotting me, I'll be eternally grateful.'

'I can do that, but on one condition. You fix me up with a date with him ASAP. Deal?'

Fen narrowed her eyes and pursed her lips. 'I don't know,' she said slowly. 'You're stiff opposition. He might not look at me twice after going out with you.'

'All's fair in love and war, kiddo.' Gail gave a confident toss of her head.

Fen regarded her in silence. She

didn't like it. She knew how attractive Gail was to the opposite sex. Fen wouldn't stand a chance against her. 'That's mean,' she sighed, and decided to appeal to her better nature. 'I thought you were my friend.'

'Hah, but I'm human too. And he looks too cute to pass up. He's poetry in motion on that bicycle.' Gail grinned.

'But you go out with lots of men.'

'Not as gorgeous as this one. So do we have a deal or shall I leave you to explain yourself to the hunk?'

Fen did not have much choice. She gave a baleful stare and gave in. 'Okay, deal. Though I don't like it.'

'And may the best woman win.'

'It's not a competition, Gail!'

'Oh, yes it is! Now get on with your exercises or you won't be dating Mr. Perfect until you're of pensionable age.'

'What a miserable thought.' Fen closed her eyes and did some deep breathing before concentrating on her leg lifts. Gritting her teeth against the pain, she slowly raised her leg and just as slowly lowered it. She did that ten times and then changed legs. That done, she lay there to allow the pain to seep away to a more manageable level.

'Asleep, Fen?'

No mistaking that low, sexy voice. Eek. James — her worst-case scenario! Fen forced herself to crank open an eye. 'James, what a nice surprise.'

James stood over her, his hands on his hips, a sheen of sweat on his glowing skin, his T-shirt glued to his hot body. He'd obviously shaken off his admirer and finished pedaling the marathon on his exercise bike. His chest rose and fell as his breathing slowed to its normal rate.

Fen felt at a total disadvantage with him towering above her. There was no way she could stand without assistance. But at least she could sit, which was better than nothing. She hauled herself upright, trying not to wince, and offered a tentative smile.

'You don't sound that surprised to

see me.' He squatted down on his haunches to be on eye level with her.

She was immediately swamped by his powerful male scent. Her senses swirled in a tumultuous whirlpool in the pit of her stomach. She could feel the heat radiating from him. If she reached out, she could touch one of those rippling biceps. She gulped and tried to focus. 'You were pointed out to me by the woman in blue.'

'That long ago? So why didn't you come and rescue me?'

'You looked as though you were doing just fine. I haven't seen you here before.' She forced a smile. 'Is this your first time?'

'Yes. I thought I'd give it a try, especially after Annabelle told me it was your local gym.'

'Annabelle?' Her voice spiked in surprise. 'How would she know?' So it wasn't fate. He'd been tracking her down! Oh Lord.

'Lynette told her.'

Her traitorous sister! 'Now I wonder

112

why they would have been discussing my gym habits?' she said, making a vow to have a serious talk with Lynette along the lines of privacy issues and the danger of giving out personal information to the likes of James McAllister's sister.

'That's easy to answer. It's because I asked them.'

'You did what? Why?' Fen felt the familiar rise of panic. Did that mean he knew why she was here? What else had he asked Annabelle to find out from Lynette? It didn't bear thinking about. 'I was in the neighborhood and wanted to see you. Mind if I use your rowing machine?' He indicated the machine situated close by.

'Go ahead. I'm not using it,' she managed to squeeze out in a strangled voice. She grappled to make sense of what he'd just said and watched in desperation as he settled himself in the rowing machine, flexing his fine muscular body. She took a deep breath. 'Why did you want to see me?' Her question came out in an undignified whoosh.

'We have unfinished business as our evening was so rudely interrupted the other night. I like you. I want to spend time with you. Is that a problem?' He flicked her a glance, his brows high in inquiry, and she had difficulty sucking in another breath.

'Yes. No. It's complicated.'

'Is there someone else?'

'No.'

'Good. That clears up one problem. So what's the complication? It can't be that bad?' He hefted the machine, effortlessly going backwards and for-wards with an easy, mechanical rhythm which was only marred by an odd clunking sound. 'Come on, Fen. Talk to me.'

Fen chewed her lower lip and wracked her brains to come up with something that would stop the conver-sation dead, because what could she say to him that wouldn't embarrass them both?

The clunking persisted. James frowned

and ceased rowing. He bent down and looked under the rowing machine. 'Grief, someone has left their crutches here.'

'Oh dear.' Fen's heart pounded into a guilty gallop. She'd momentarily forgotten the hidden crutches. Was there no end to the afternoon's awkwardness?

'I wonder who?' He glanced around the gym. 'They can't get very far without them so they should be easy to spot.' He smiled easily at Fen.

She tried to mold her lips in a return smile, but was doubtful how successful she was.

'I'll take those, thank you Mr. McAllister.' Gail jogged up out of nowhere and popped the crutches under one arm.

'Are they for the clients who have overdone it?' James grinned.

'We like to provide a full service,' responded Gail, her voice full of warmth. 'Let me know if I can be of any assistance. We would like to make your first time at our gymnasium a satisfactory experience and one to be repeated — often.'

'I shall, thanks,' said James.

'You never said that to me on my first day, Gail,' said Fen, trying not to feel jealous of her friend's reaction to James, though she couldn't blame her. James was special. 'You're giving him preferential treatment.'

'And wouldn't you in my position?' Gail beamed.

Fen rolled her eyes.

'Well, wouldn't you?' asked James, quirking a slightly lopsided grin at Fen.

'I told you, I don't play favorites.' She ran a hand through her hair in what she hoped was a nonchalant manner and avoided his eyes. She'd never wanted to play favorites more — with James and herself top of the list! But of course, she couldn't.

'Wish you did, sweetheart,' he said.

Fen's heart did a double somersault at the unexpected endearment.

Gail raised her fine brows and regarded Fen with keen interest.

Fen's face flushed and she panicked. 'Okay, I will play favorites,' she announced, her voice breathless all of a sudden. She was rewarded by a deeper smile from James. 'As you two are among my most favorite clients, I'll tee up a date between you. How about tonight?'

'Yep,' said Gail promptly. 'I'm free. Sounds great.'

The smile froze on James' face. His eyes narrowed.

Uh-oh. He wasn't happy. Fen could see the war between good manners and anger flickering across his face. Good manners won out.

'I'll be delighted,' said James. 'But you must realize . . . er . . . ?'

'Gail,' said Gail.

'Gail, I have actually resigned from Fen's agency so I'm not available for other dates.'

'Oh.' She pouted. 'What a pity.'

'Have you resigned?' said Fen, her brain a muddle of confusion. He'd resigned and reinstated himself one too many times for her to keep tabs.

'Yes,' he said firmly. 'But I shall be

extremely happy to meet you tonight, Gail. It'll be a great pleasure.'

'That's settled then,' said Fen, trying to keep the satisfaction out of her voice. 'Why don't you go with Gail now and organize things so you don't forget?'

'But I was just getting into my stride on the rowing machine.' James shook his head. 'I haven't worked up a decent sweat yet.'

Fen's eyes dropped involuntarily to his damp T-shirt. Any damper and it would be transparent. Well, there was a thought she shouldn't be having!

'Come along, James,' said Gail. 'While things are quiet.'

'And the machine will still be here in five minutes,' said Fen, who was pleased to see Gail had casually popped the crutches back down on the floor near to Fen's mat, just out of James' sight line.

James continued to hover over Fen as if he couldn't bear to leave her, which gave her a sneaking thrill — not that she would admit it to anyone else. 'Go away, James. You're intimidating me. I can't exercise with you breathing down my neck.'

'But I want to see you go through your paces.' He gave her a suggestive wink.

'It's not a pretty sight.'

'Let me be the judge of that.'

'Take him away, Gail.'

'With pleasure,' said the other woman, who linked her arm through James'. 'This way, sir.'

As soon as they were out of sight, Fen picked up the crutches and swung herself towards the changing rooms and relative safety. Once inside, she plonked herself down on the bench and breathed a sigh of relief. A close call, but now what? She really must do a workout, but not while James was around. That would be out of the question.

Ten minutes later, Gail poked her head around the changing room door. 'He's looking for you,' she said. 'And asked me to check in here.'

'Pretend I've gone,' said Fen.

'Are you sure?' Gail's eyes widened. 'He seems awfully keen.'

'Very sure.'

'Be it on your head, Fen.'

'I can cope with any fall-out,' she said with more bravado than confidence. 'What's the worst he could do? Bawl me out for leaving without saying goodbye? I'm a big girl, Gail. Everything will be fine.'

6

Fen drowsily flaked out in front of the television, watching a re-run of an old sitcom. The hour was late but she was too comfortable to switch off the TV and hobble to bed. Once James had disappeared from the gym, she'd spent a strenuous hour and a half going through her regime and now she was pooped. Absolutely.

Her mind wandered for the six millionth time away from the comedy show to wonder about James and Gail. How were they getting on? Was there a spark of attraction? She didn't really want to think about them getting cozy together, but they probably would, wouldn't they? They were both beautiful people, both single; it was almost a dead cert that this date could lead to other things.

Rats.

Of course, Gail was a trifle shorter than James' usual slender but statuesque Gorgeous Gazelles, but she was a stunner in a robust, Nordic sort of way. She had been very popular among Fen's male clients and there'd be no surprise if James became as captivated as the rest of them. She'd be more surprised if he wasn't.

And Gail had said she was very, very interested in him. While she made Fen slog her way through various leg-strengthening exercises, she'd chatted on about how much she was looking forward to their date, how great it would be getting to know him, how charming and handsome he was. Of course, she didn't have to tell Fen all that. Fen was more than aware of James' attractions, which made avoiding him all the more poignant.

James was special. No disputing that. And he was worming his way into Fen's heart with a rapidity that did little for her peace of mind. It wasn't fair. It was a dirty rotten conspiracy that Fen wasn't in the position to do something about it.

She must have dozed off because it took her a moment to realize that her doorbell was ringing.

'Coming,' she called in a sleep-groggy voice and hobbled her way towards the door, supporting herself with various pieces of furniture. 'Who is it?'

'It's me.'

James? Uh-oh. Fen cracked the door open. 'What's wrong? Where's Gail?'

'May I come in?'

Her gaze searched the hallway. 'What have you done with her?'

'I'll explain over a coffee.'

Omigod, if she let him in he'd see her limping. 'No way. It's late.'

'You're still dressed.'

'Yes, but I was about to go to bed.' And he'd want to know why she was limping and she would have to come up with an explanation. Fast!

'Fen, please. I need to talk to you.'

He sounded so little-boy-lost that Fen's resolve crumpled like a hot air balloon deprived of gas. And it was awfully tempting to spend some time with him. 'Okay, but only a quick drink. I'm rather tired.'

He followed her into the small apartment. Fen grabbed the sideboard and then the back of the chair as she made her way towards her tiny kitchen, hoping he wouldn't notice her awkward progress. But to her consternation he did.

'Are you all right?' His voice was laced with concern.

'Yes, I . . . er . . . overdid my workout in the gym today.'

'You weren't exactly flat out when I saw you. In fact, I reckon you left early. Why? Because of me?'

He had a hurt air about him and Fen felt like a heel. 'You? Rubbish. I had other commitments. But I did return later to do some more. I must have got too carried away.' If Fen hadn't been holding on to the kitchen counter, she would have crossed her fingers. She hoped God wasn't out with his lightning bolts to strike her down, but what could a girl say under the circumstances?

'I see.'

She hoped he didn't. 'Black or white coffee?'

'White, two sugars.'

James carried the tray through to the living room and set the hot drinks down on the low coffee table.

Fen settled herself on her old three-seater couch, hoping he'd take the armchair.

He didn't but promptly sat right next to her.

Fen experienced a rash of tingles. He was too close. 'You'll probably find the chair more comfortable than this old thing.'

'I'm fine here.' He handed her a coffee.

Fen cradled it between both hands and blew on the steamy surface. 'So didn't things work out with Gail?' she asked with what she hoped was casual nonchalance.

'We had a great time.'

'Oh.' How great, she wanted to know but wasn't game to ask. Instead, she said, 'I'm glad.' She wondered if she sounded sincere enough.

'But . . . '

'There's a but?' Her spirits lifted.

'Yes. Definitely a but. I won't be seeing her again. There *was* a problem, you see.'

'A problem with Gail? I don't believe you. Gail is one of my most popular girls on file. I never have problems finding her a date and she gets a lot of repeat dates too. So what's the deal?'

James smiled. 'To put it simply, she's not you, Fen.'

Fen had chosen that moment to take a sip of coffee. The scalding liquid went down much too fast in response to his surprising admission. She spluttered like a strangled chicken.

James whipped the mug out of her hands and placed it back on the tray. He then rubbed her back to help ease the choking.

It didn't help. Having his hand rubbing up and down her spine was causing greater difficulties. She tried to wave him away.

'Would you like a glass of water?'

'No, thanks,' she gasped. 'I'll be fine in a moment.' Fen wiped the tears from her eyes and then gave James a frustrated look. He had no right to come out with little gems like that, especially when she'd just taken a mouthful of coffee. And he shouldn't touch her! He made her all shivery and hot, inside and out. 'So what are you doing here?'

'I wanted to see you.'

His words were bittersweet and made her want to weep. 'James, I've told you before,' she said, her voice wobbling. 'I am not available for dating.'

'And I'm not available for your agency dating.'

'Okay.' But it wasn't okay. There was a sharp pain in her heart. A missing warmth in her belly. A sense of loss pounding in her head. If James stayed on her books there would be an excuse to spar with him. Without that common ground, there was no reason to call him, no chance to talk to him, meet with him. 'Which means we won't be seeing each other,' she said, a slight catch in her voice betraying her disappointment.

His brows rose a fraction. 'I don't think it changes anything between us, sweetheart.' He leaned towards her, reaching for her hand, holding it in the secure strength of his. 'Except we'll have more time together without the constraints of your strict agency rules.' His lips twitched into a teasing smile.

'You don't understand,' she said, imploring him to anyway. She tugged away her hand, but he recaptured it easily.

His smile faded. 'No, you don't understand, Fenella Grant. You're stuck with me in your life. Get used to it.' Strong and firm, his tone brooked no argument.

'Oh.' Warmth flooded through her, in

spite of her good intentions to keep him at a distance. How could she not feel thrilled by his words? But however much James made her heart flutter, she had to be strong for the both of them. Because a relationship couldn't work between them. Ever. But Fen didn't know what she could say without sounding rude.

James, still holding her hand, said, 'You have a nice place.'

'Thank you.' She knew he was giving her time to adjust to the shift in their relationship. Not that it would make any difference.

He stood and prowled around her airy living room.

She looked at it as he might be seeing the space. She'd chosen the ground floor flat because of the big front room. In her dancing days, she had used the space to exercise and rehearse dance routines. There was still a *barre* attached to one wall for her warm-up routines which had included exercises such as *pliés* and *relevés*. She still used the room for exercise, but nothing as graceful or rewarding as ballet. Just the basics to get her to walk again unaided.

'You like ballet.' The three words were a statement, not a question.

Fen squirmed further down into the soft sofa cushions and hid her disquiet by burying her nose in her mug. 'Yes,' she said awkwardly. She couldn't deny it. Her walls were covered with pictures of the various roles she had undertaken as well as photos of her favorite dancers. Her collection of advertising show posters over the years were scattered in the mix. She prayed he wouldn't look too closely at her personal photographs.

But he was contrary. She knew that and wasn't overly surprised when the very first picture James picked up was a black-and-white, framed photograph taken when she was sixteen. The picture was one of her favorites where she'd struck the classic ballerina pose, her head slightly inclined, her hands crossed gracefully across her breasts.

With her hair swept into a tight bun, her face was revealed in its glory. Accented by stage make-up, her lips were full of hidden promise and her eyes were deep, dark mysterious pools of emotion. The photo was taken just before her first major professional role when she'd danced Swan Lake at the Theatre Royal in Brighton.

James studied the silver-framed picture for several minutes. 'She's beautiful,' he said. Then he frowned, his eyes thoughtful. 'She looks familiar but I can't quite place her. Is she very famous?'

Fen's throat constricted, her chest squeezing as though tight steel bands of fire were clamping around her fragile body. Blood thrummed in her head and she was dangerously close to being sick.

'Not anymore,' she said, forcing her vocal cords to work even though her throat was closing with unshed tears.

'And who is this? The same dancer?'

The photo was taken two years later when she was dancing the part of

Giselle in Paris. 'Yes, the same girl.'

'She's gorgeous. Do you know her personally? Is that why you're such a fan?'

'Yes.' She dug her nails into her hand to stop herself from shouting at him. But then he didn't know how much he was hurting her.

'You should sign her up for your agency. She'd be the most popular babe on the block.'

Definite torture. She had to make him stop. 'She's not interested,' she forced out.

'Shame. Now even *I'd* be tempted to maintain my membership if there was the chance of dating her.' He laughed and threw Fen a saucy glance, inviting her to join in the joke.

Fen could feel her heart breaking. He fancied her old, pre-accident self. How would he react if he knew the girl in the photo was Fen? She had been right to keep her accident secret. She couldn't bear to suffer his pity, see the sympathy in his eyes and the cooling of his attraction for her.

'You wouldn't be her type,' she said with repressive bluntness and then added, 'There are some chocolate biscuits in the cupboard if you're hungry.'

'No, thanks. I just had dinner with Gail, remember?'

'As if I could forget,' she muttered to herself. 'Where did you go?' Time she steered him on to another, safer subject.

The ruse worked. He told her about the small bistro where they'd eaten. It led to a discussion of Fen and James' favorite restaurants. Most of James' were of places way above Fen's touch. To her, it emphasized how different they were, how far apart their worlds. It'd been sheer fluke their paths had ever crossed in the first instance and it wouldn't be long, in her opinion, that those paths would veer away again. They would then continue on their separate life journeys.

'We must go out for dinner one

night,' said James with far too much enthusiasm for Fen's comfort. 'And I'll treat you to my most favorite restaurant.'

'After Christmas.' That would give Fen more time to cook up a good excuse not to go.

'Why not sooner?'

'It's all a bit hectic what with the holiday and stuff,' she said.

'Shame. There must be a way I can persuade you.'

'No.' It was time to change the subject again and she'd been more than intrigued with what had caused the crookedness of his nose. It gave him such a disreputable air amid all his suave, man-about-town-ness. Now seemed the perfect time to ask him. 'Tell me, how did you break your nose?'

'My nose?' James gave it a cursory rub. 'Ah. Back in my youth I was a gung-ho horse rider. I entered cross-country events and one day came a cropper, landing smack on my face.'

Fen shuddered. She could sympathize as her own face had taken the brunt of her fall in the hit-and-run accident.

'I smashed up my face, broke my nose and collar bone, lost a couple of teeth and busted my jaw,' James catalogued with cool matter-of-factness.

'Ouch. That would have hurt.' Fen winced, feeling his bygone pain with an acuteness born of experience.

'My pride more than anything. I was trying too hard to impress a girl.' He laughed and shook his head in self-deprecation.

'How did she react to your accident?' Fen asked, more than a little curious.

'Well,' James twisted his mouth. 'She did come and see me in hospital but I wasn't looking very pretty. She couldn't handle my cut and swollen face. There were no kiss-it-betters or comforting hugs. Instead she was derogatory about my horsemanship. I think she thought I was a loser.' He shrugged. 'After that one perfunctory visit, I didn't hear from her again.'

'She wasn't worth it then,' Fen stated, appalled at the girl's tactlessness and hurting for the bruised heart of an impressionable youth.

'True. It was a good lesson to learn. Have you ever ridden, Fen?'

'No.'

'But your sister rides. She goes hacking with Annabelle every week. I thought all girls in the country rode.'

'A lot do. But I don't. Horseback riding involves different muscles.' It was a throwaway comment and one she immediately regretted.

'I beg your pardon?'

Fen wished she'd swallowed her tongue. That was the trouble relaxing around James. Now she'd have to explain. 'I was dancing mad. If I'd ridden horses I would have developed different muscles which wouldn't have helped my dancing.'

'Do you still dance?' His gaze scanned the room again.

'No.'

Her flat tone made James glance back, a slight frown between his brows. 'Why?'

'One of those things,' she hedged and pretended to smother a yawn.

'You're tired. I best let you go to bed.'

Fen winced as she tried to stand.

'Are you okay?'

'Stiff muscles, that's all. Nothing a good hot soak in a Radox bath won't cure.' She wished it could be that simple, that her legs could be healed so easily rather than enduring hour upon hour of grueling physiotherapy.

'Don't come to the door. Save those legs.' James leaned over and cupped her face in his hands. He took one long look at her and then kissed her softly on the lips.

Fen's stomach did a spontaneous meltdown and turned to mush. Her blood fizzed like shaken lemonade on a hot day. If such a small kiss could produce such results, what would a full-blown one do to her system?

She'd probably implode!

'Night, Fen,' he said with warm gentleness.

'Night.' To her disgust her voice came out as a whisper.

She heard the front door shut and sat there for a good five minutes to savor that sweetest of kisses and to regret things couldn't develop further. How could she keep on seeing him?

But how could she not?

She knew she was falling in love and there wasn't anything she could do about it.

Damn her lame legs. Damn the accident. And damn James McAllister for making her feel again.

She struggled to the bathroom and turned on the shower. As she waited for the water to heat up, she stared with brutal frankness at herself in the mirror.

Where was the girl of the photographs? She was barely visible. When the car had knocked her over, Fen had fallen face first on to the pavement. She had smashed her cheekbones and broken her jaw. The surgeons had had to reconstruct her face. The elfin oval of yesteryear was now a flatter version. The high cheekbones less prominent, the eyes slightly wider and more almond-shaped than before, the jaw more rounded. Her spiky short hair made a big difference too. Once it grew again, perhaps her features would be softened. She could at least try.

She wasn't ugly, now that the swelling and scarring had faded, but she wasn't the pert beauty staring out of the photographs.

As she stared, the steam from the hot water began to fog up the glass. Best thing too. There was no point in crying over what couldn't be.

7

'You are coming to my Christmas bash, aren't you, Fen?' Lucinda chirped down the phone line. 'It's gonna be bigger and better than usual. I've invited everyone who's anyone.'

Fen winced. A huge, noisy party. Oh no. Lucinda's annual, end-of-year affairs for all those involved in her chain of travel agencies were a legend that could only be endured if one felt on top of things. She didn't. 'I might give it a miss this year.' There was no 'might' about it. Fen had no intention of going. She clutched the receiver hard, hoping she'd be strong enough to resist Lucinda's arguments.

'But you missed last year's party, too,' Lucinda grumbled.

'I couldn't help it! I was stuck in a hospital bed with my legs in traction.'

'Well, you're not this time so there's

no excuse. Come on, Fen, it'll be fun. There's going to be music and food and plenty of grog. You can't not come.'

Lucinda didn't often plead, but she was shoveling it on in huge portions. 'It's not really my scene,' protested Fen.

'It used to be.'

'Things have changed. You might not have noticed, Lucinda, darling, but I can't dance anymore.'

'You could shuffle if some nice man held you up,' Lucinda wheedled.

'Sounds perfect.' Fen didn't try to keep the sarcasm out of her tone.

'Anyway, dancing is such a small part of the night. Lots of people won't be dancing. They'll be eating, drinking and skulking off to dark corners for a bit of a snog.'

'No, thanks,' Fen shuddered. 'I'm not into kissing in dark corners.'

'You can join the wallflowers, then.'

'Thanks a bunch.'

'Come on, Fen!' Lucinda's tone of voice rose. 'You love a good party. When was the last time you went to one?'

'Actually, it was last week.' James' fortieth birthday — and hadn't that turned out to be a night to remember. The memory of his kiss was still giving her palpitations.

'And it was a blast, right?' said the other woman.

'Wrong. I couldn't wait to leave.' Actually, she would have loved to have stayed and danced within the circle of his strong, muscular arms, but her wretched, stupid lame legs . . .

'Well, this will be different. We'll all be swinging. There will be loads of people there. Lots of old friends. Don't be such a party pooper. It's almost Christmas.'

In the end, Fen allowed herself to be browbeaten. Much easier to give in than to suffer Lucinda's constant nagging. And anyway, it wasn't as if she'd be bumping into James there.

★　★　★

She entered the nightclub late. Already the party was in full swing. The men

142

were in suits, the women in a rainbow of different colors and designs, some modest and others showing plenty of flesh. Fen had chosen a long, figure-hugging black sequined dress that covered her from neck to toe and hid any traces of scars. She thought it would help her blend into the background and didn't realize until it was too late that the dress increased her allure a thousand-fold.

She maneuvered herself on her crutches towards the bar. She planned to sit there, as unobtrusively as possible, and leave after a polite period of time. But she hadn't taken into account the fact that her friends would be pleased to see her after her self-imposed exile.

'Hey, Fen!' said one, and 'Look who's here!' exclaimed another; and within minutes she was surrounded by a bunch of fast-talking, delighted women and sharing months of gossip.

Deep into recounting a particularly funny incident, Fen suddenly heard her name spoken in a soft, endearing manner that sent a warm shiver across her nerve endings. Abruptly abandoning the story and twisting on her bar stool, she glanced behind her and almost slipped off the stool and into an ungainly heap on the floor. She swallowed hard. 'James! What are you doing here?'

'Don't sound so thrilled!' he said a smidge defensively. But then he smiled and leaned forward to kiss her on the cheek.

Just the touch and smell of him sent her nerves jitterbugging. 'Well, gosh,' she said trying to think through the sudden red haze of longing which enveloped her in a rush. One small kiss did this to her? She was a sad case! 'I didn't expect to see you again this side of Christmas,' she gabbled.

'Lucinda invited me.'

Lucinda! That brought her back to earth. *Well, of course Lucinda had!* Fen had introduced the two of them, so why hadn't she considered the possibility that Lucinda might invite James to her party? Lucinda had been smitten with him since their initial date and had asked Fen on several occasions for a repeat performance. But James had said he couldn't stand the woman, so why had he accepted the invite?

'I thought you wanted to stay clear of Lucinda. Considered her bad for your health given her appetite for men? Or were you just feeding me a line?' Fen suspected she sounded snitchy, but couldn't help herself.

James held up his hands. 'Hold on, my sweet. Not so fast. I voluntarily stepped into the man-eater's lair because I knew you'd be here. You're the reason, Fen. The only one.'

'Oh.' That sounded good. Fen almost began to bask in the glow of knowing she held that sort of allure for him, but then a nasty thought popped into her head. What had Lucinda done with her crutches? James mustn't see them.

'You don't look overjoyed to see me,' he said, his eyes still shimmering with a defensive gleam.

'Of course I am.' Quickly she reassured him, reaching out to touch his hand, then withdrawing it, fast. She was too tempted to cling to him and never let go. 'I'm always pleased to see you, James.'

She made hasty introductions to those circling her. Maybe one of her more forward girlfriends would whisk him off to the dance floor so she could find her crutches and make her escape. Where was Lucinda when you needed her?

'Shall we dance?' James asked Fen, his hand on her elbow, forestalling any other invitations.

Fen sought around for a plausible excuse, struggling against the panic whisking through her veins. Her gaze alighted on a glass of wine that wasn't hers. That would do. 'I'd love to,' she said. 'But I think I've had one too many. My legs feel wobbly.'

'I'm shocked.' James chuckled. 'But not deterred. How about I hold you up and we shuffle very slowly together? I shan't let you fall, darling. Promise.'

The intimate endearment pierced her defense and crumbled her resolve. Was it possible to enjoy a dance with him? Have his arms around her in a close embrace? Tempting. Oh, ever so tempting. Fen nibbled her bottom lip and then made a decision. 'Okay,' she said, doubt and fear and longing adding to the panic and making a churning cocktail in her tummy. 'But I'm warning you, don't let go!'

He eased her off the stool and placed a supporting arm around her waist.

'You're going to dance?' asked her friend Marie. Her surprise threatened to unnerve Fen further.

'Just watch us and be amazed,' said Fen, shooting her a warning glance. She prayed Marie wouldn't say anything revealing and drop Fen in trouble.

Marie gave her the thumbs up and said, 'I shall. Well done, Fen. Way to go.'

'What was all that about?' asked James as he drew her into his arms on the dance floor.

'She . . . er . . . knows how much I've had,' she ad-libbed.

'A night for letting your hair down, is it?'

'If I had any hair to let down.' Fen bit on a laugh.

'Yes, you do keep it short.' He boldly ran his hand over her scalp.

Fen shivered deliciously as his caress caused a shot of liquid fire to streak through her body. 'I do,' she managed to breathe through the heat.

'But it's very endearing, in a pixie-sort of way.' His tone was teasing.

'I'm glad you approve.'

'Totally. As I do with everything about you.' And now he sounded serious.

Fen rolled her eyes to show her disbelief but couldn't help feeling flattered anyway. It was wonderful to receive compliments. They were so rare nowadays.

People packed the dance floor and James held her close in the protective arc of his arms. They moved with infinitesimal motion to the soft strains of the smoochy melody. The sensation was bliss. Fen had so missed dancing, so missed being held in an intimate embrace by a man who made her feel feminine, beautiful and desirable.

Of course, it was all an illusion. The magical moment would be over in a couple of minutes. But for those few precious minutes she gave herself up to this gorgeous man and the beautiful music, pretending once again she was a graceful ballerina instead of a lumbering cripple.

Her eyes closed, she swayed in time, letting the music seep into her bones, letting James' warmth feed her starved soul. It felt so good having his arms around her, one hand on her waist, the other firmly on her hip.

And then she felt his lips on her hair, whispering caressing words of silky seduction and endearment at her temple.

'You're so warm and inviting, sweetheart,' he murmured, his breath an exquisite caress in itself. 'You feel so good. So soft. I just want to fold you close so you can feel the vibration of my heart against yours and realize exactly what you do to me . . . '

Fen's eyes flew open, ready to protest, but then immediately fluttered shut. Why stop him? This moment was hers to enjoy and she'd treasure it for as long as it took.

The music stopped after what felt a lifetime. Fen stood there in the circle of his arms, totally supported by James, their hearts beating in time, their pulses thundering the same heated rhythm. She forced her eyelids open again and stared up into his handsome face, not even registering his crooked nose.

'Are you game to keep dancing, Ms. Grant?' he whispered, a tender smile curving his lips as well as warming his eyes.

'If you're game to keep me upright, Mr. McAllister,' she said, smiling back.

'You can stay in my arms for eternity

and it still wouldn't be long enough,' he murmured.

Her heart sang at his words. 'Think you can seduce me with your silver tongue?' she gently teased.

'But it's true. I love holding you close. It feels so right.'

'Your arms would soon tire,' she said, trying to keep a little perspective in their dealings or she'd be in danger of melting on the spot.

'Never. And as for seducing you, I don't need words for that.' His lips brushed her pale brow and she shivered in delight. He then found her ear lobe and gently nipped it, sending spirals of warmth curling through her body. She couldn't help but moan it felt so good. His lips moved to her neck and he nuzzled and bit the delicate pale flesh. Exquisite torture. He bit again and Fen gasped.

'James! Behave yourself. We're in a public place.' But she didn't want him to stop. It felt too delicious having his teeth graze her skin and suckle the spot where her pulse pounded for want of him.

'Ah, yes, but you're in my embrace and at my mercy,' he said with a lightness tinged with a husky bass note. 'Tonight you're all mine.' His arms tightened, molding her body to his, sending ripples of heat through to her inner soul. She'd never felt such an intoxicating sensation.

'James!'

But he ignored her plea. His questing lips descended on hers and melded in a white hot heat that infused into every atom of her body — a body responding to him at every level: heart, mind and soul.

Her heart skittered, her pulses clamoring and the heat low down in her belly gathering steam. 'James . . . ' she whimpered, incredulous at the speed and depth of their unexpected passion.

'Hush, baby.' His voice was hoarse and tense with the same desire spellbinding her.

'James,' she said again. 'We can't

. . . We mustn't . . . You have to stop . . . I didn't realize it could be like this . . . '

'Ssh. I know, sweetheart. Neither did I. Just relax.' His hold subtly changed. Less intense, less passionate, more nurturing and protective, but still incredibly romantic to Fen nonetheless.

They danced on for a few more musical numbers to allow their heartbeats to ease to a more sedate rhythm. But the whole experience was slow and sensual, and Fen was acutely aware she was drowning in overwhelming love and desire for this man.

But these feelings would never do.

Not while she couldn't walk. It was unfair on the both of them.

But tonight was hers.

Suddenly their dancing was interrupted. An exuberant and tipsy Lucinda, in a too-tight and short red Lycra dress with big hair and bold make-up, made the DJ stop the music. She wrested away the microphone so she could deliver a flamboyant speech.

'Darlings,' she said. 'I want to take this moment to wish all of you, my family, friends, lovers, cripples, work colleagues and hangers-on — you know which category you fall in — a very merry Christmas and to charge you to bring me all your travel and holiday business in the New Year. Have a great party.' She hiccoughed, returned the microphone and left the stage on the arm of a young man.

'Well, I must fall into the hangers-on category,' said James with a rueful grin as the music resumed. 'How about you, Fen?'

'She's definitely one of the cripples,' said a smart-mouthed acquaintance dancing nearby with Gail. Gail smacked his shoulder.

Fen forced a laugh. 'I think I fall into a couple of those pigeonholes.' She avoided making eye contact with James in case he saw her stricken expression. The magic was broken. Time to leave.

Later, back at the bar, she managed to organize going home with one of her friends without James' knowledge.

'Stay,' he insisted when he heard of the arrangement. 'I'll take you home later.'

'Sorry, but this has been arranged for some time,' she lied. 'I'm staying the night. We're having a girls' sleepover.'

'What a waste.'

Fen playfully punched him on the arm. 'Not at all. Nothing was going to happen anyway,' she said with a wide smile, knowing full well *anything* could have happened between them after those chemistry-packed dances.

'That's what you think,' he muttered in frustration. 'You can't ignore what went on between us just now, Fen. We were dynamite together.'

Eek. They sure were. 'I'm not ignoring anything. But plans have been made and I don't break my promises. Good night, James.'

* * *

James watched Fen and two of her friends weave their way through the partygoers. Her friends, their arms twined around Fen's slim waist, steered her towards the door without incident. He had a sudden flashback to when Lynette and her husband escorted her away from his party. Had she had too much to drink then too? He shook his head in bemusement. What a case she was. She hadn't struck him as being drunk. He hadn't smelt any alcohol on her breath when he'd kissed her full, soft lips. She hadn't drunk anything since he'd been there, turning down all offers of wine. In fact, he'd have sworn on his grandmother's grave Fenella Grant was stone cold sober.

'She doesn't seem drunk,' he said to no one in particular.

'Who?' said Marie, the woman who'd congratulated Fen on dancing. She was propping up the bar, close to James.

'Fen.'

'Fenella Grant? Drunk? You must be kidding.' Marie laughed and shook her head.

James turned towards her. 'Excuse

me? Am I missing something here?'

'By the sound of it, yes! Fen doesn't drink much. Hardly ever touches the stuff.'

Exactly what he thought. 'But she said . . . '

The girl cocked her head to one side and regarded him thoughtfully. 'How well do you know Fen?'

'We met a couple of weeks ago.'

'So you don't actually *know* much about her?' She pushed.

'No, I guess not.' Though not through lack of trying. But she'd always given the impression she was stonewalling him when he'd attempted to learn more about her. As if it didn't matter if he knew zilch about her. But he wanted to know every single thing about Fenella Grant.

James found her evasiveness frustrating. He wasn't used to being the one doing all the chasing in a relationship. Usually women actively encouraged him to get involved. Sometimes too much. But Fen was different. So, her reticence challenged to his ego. But now he'd gone beyond being piqued. Fen was lodged under his skin, had burrowed into his heart and there was no going back — for either of them.

'Perhaps you should make it your business to find out,' Marie said with a slight smile. 'You could be in for a surprise.'

'Meaning?'

'It's not for me to say.' She primly closed her mouth and pretended to zipper it shut.

'Is it something I'm not going to like?'

The woman's stare was direct. 'Depends how much you care for her.'

I care, thought James. I care very deeply. Just what is Ms. Fenella Grant's dark secret?

★ ★ ★

Another night, another party and Fen sighed. She was fed up. She pulled on a straight black skirt with a back slit and sparkly top. She carelessly daubed on some make-up and then eyed herself critically in the mirror. She looked pale and washed out thanks to a bad night tossing and turning in bed thinking about James, wanting him there with her. Lust had replaced pain as the source of her wakefulness. She supposed she should be grateful, but both made awful bedfellows!

She was worried about lying to James. How long could she continue to hoodwink him? Last night had been an extremely close call. One of these days he would find out that she was lame and then who knew what would happen.

She swiped on another layer of mascara and added a little mauve eye shadow. Her eyes blinked back, now large and dark and a little too top-heavy for her lighter make-up. She reapplied to address the balance and then put more gel on her hair. She had another squizz in the mirror. Oh dear. Her appearance wasn't improving.

Now she wasn't waif-like, but more Goth!

There wasn't time to wipe off the excess cosmetics. The taxi had already hooted once. Fen collected her bag and went to grab her crutches. Her hand hovered. Why not try out the walking stick? Her legs were getting stronger. The stick would be less obtrusive. She was almost ready to downsize her walking aids anyway. Why not start tonight? With a spurt of new-found confidence, she snatched up the rose-wood stick.

She was halfway to the front door when her leg gave out. The stick slipped from under her and Fen came down heavily, catching her eye on the corner of the coffee table.

Intense, gut-wrenching agony streaked through her. She gave a sharp scream and shrank into a tight, fetal ball, clutching her eye in one hand and leg in the other. The pain was bad, rippling through her wave after wave. She groaned long and hard and then gritted her teeth, willing the torment to go away with every ounce of her strength. Nausea swamped her, causing beads of cold sweat to sheen her skin. Gradually, slowly, the sharpness morphed into a hard, throbbing knot that was slightly more bearable. Just.

She didn't know how long she'd lain there but she was roused by the doorbell, which rang once, twice, three times.

Tentatively, Fen removed her hand and looked at it. Thank goodness, there was no blood. A gaping wound on top of the sick pain would have been the pits. But her stomach still churned and a few more moments passed before she gathered enough reserve to crawl to the door.

With great determination, she hauled herself to her feet. Favoring her stronger leg, she balanced and opened the door to the cabbie, preparing to send him away. There was no way she would go out now. Intense, pounding pain in both her eye and leg made her feel she was going to throw up at any moment. She flung open the door.

Her breath caught in her throat. Instead of the cabbie standing on the steps, it was James.

'Good lord, Fen, what's happened?' he blurted out, scooping her into the circle of his arms, holding her warm and secure against his chest.

Fen experienced a split moment of disbelief, followed by sheer panic, which then gave way to relief. She was safe. She sagged against him and the floodgates opened and she sobbed into his shoulder.

'The taxi . . . ' she managed to say through her tears. 'He's waiting.'

'I've sent him off. As we're going to the same party, I thought we could go together.'

'Same party?' She could barely concentrate on what he was saying. The effort of standing sent the pain riding over her and through her. Sweat prickled on her dampened skin and blackness pressed in, ready to engulf her. She knew the symptoms: she was going to faint.

James' voice came from a long way off. 'Gail's party, right? But what's happened?' He pulled back to look at her.

She still shielded her eye but the effort to keep upright was almost killing her. 'I fell and hit my eye. You're going to Gail's?' She tried to sound coherent but struggled to keep functioning, and she staggered as the nausea and blackness rode her hard.

'Forget the party. Let's look at your eye.' He began to move her away from the door.

Her leg could stand the strain no longer and buckled. The darkness caved in.

James caught her before she fell. 'You've injured your leg too?'

His distant, muffled voice sounded as if he was a long, long way away. She nodded, her eyes full of tears, her teeth biting down hard on her lower lip so she wouldn't cry out. 'Feel faint,' she managed to mumble at last.

'Hell, Fen. Put your head between your knees.' He had her on the floor and was pushing her head down. The pain in her eye was awful, but the blood flow soon returned to her brain.

'Better?' said James after a space of several minutes.

She nodded, not trusting her voice.

'Well, let's get you more comfortable.' He picked her up and carried her through to the living room, placing her on the couch, being careful not to jar her. 'I'll go and get a cold cloth. You stay put.'

As if she could move, thought Fen with black bitterness. Where was the stick? It must have skidded under the chair. Thank goodness the crutches were out of sight in the bedroom. But those facts were all incidental. She had to fight this pain before it consumed her and reduced her to a blubbering wreck.

'Do you want a cold press for your leg too?' he asked when he came back and knelt beside her.

'No.' She shivered and pressed a hand to her mouth. 'A bucket,' she demanded. 'Quick. Under the sink. I'm going to be sick.'

James raced off. There was the sound of cupboard doors opening and slamming. He was back in a few seconds and pressed the bucket into her arms.

Not Fen's finest moment, but she was beyond caring. At least after vomiting, she felt a little better. 'Sorry,' she mumbled.

James retrieved the bucket. 'No problem, sweetheart.' He stroked her cheek. 'I'm glad I was here for you. That must have been some fall you took.' He lifted the flannel and studied her eye. 'You're going to have a shiner. It's already turning purple.'

'Probably looks worse than it is. My eye-shadow is mauve.' She gave a weak, watery laugh.

'Well, it might explain some of the technicolor, but the eye still looks bad.'

Feeling rather embarrassed, she said,

'I'll be okay. Honest.'

'I'm not so sure. How about I take you to casualty and have you checked out?'

'No. No hospitals,' she said quickly, panic underscoring her words.

'Don't like hospitals, eh? Not that I can blame you. But I do think we should get you looked at.'

'No, James, please. You'd better get off to Gail's party or you'll miss all the fun.' First Lucinda's party, now Gail's. Fen was so glad she'd introduced him to her friends! There was no avoiding him on this year's Christmas party circuit.

'If you think I'm leaving you, think again.'

'But I'll be fine.' She attempted to smile, but she could feel her lips wobble, so she waved him away with her hand. 'I'll take a couple of painkillers and head to bed. I really don't feel like being social.'

'Do you have any tablets?'

Did she have tablets! She told him

where they were.

James headed for her medicine cabinet in the bathroom. He came back with a packet of painkillers in one hand and a glass of water in the other. 'You've got a stack of medication back there. Are you thinking of opening your own drug dispensing service?' he asked as he watched her swallow the white pills.

Oh no. Fen had forgotten her place resembled a pharmacy. She'd tried not to use them, hence such a buildup. James must think her a total disaster. 'I like to be prepared,' she improvised. 'Feel free to go now. I'll just rest here.'

James took the cold pack off her eye. 'I'm not leaving. You might have concussion or something. People don't throw up after a small fall. I'm not taking any chances.'

'My pain threshold isn't very good. I'm a sook.'

'Sook or not, I'm not going.'

'Please,' she whimpered. 'I just want to sleep. Reaction to the fall, I guess.'

Go, just go, she wailed inwardly.

James compressed his lips and stared for a moment. 'I'll compromise,' he said eventually. 'I'll get you to bed and then see how you are once you're safely tucked in for the night. I don't want you keeling over again on that gammy leg. You may do yourself some further damage.'

Gammy leg? He knew! Fen's heart sank. But then she realized he meant the leg she'd just fallen on. Phew.

James carried her through to the bedroom and laid her on the double bed. He quirked an eyebrow. 'Need a hand getting changed?' he asked.

She heard the humorous inflexion in his voice. 'I can manage from now on,' she replied and was disgusted to hear the words tremble. His touch was causing her body to tremble too. It had nothing on an aspen leaf in a stiff lakeside breeze. Hopefully James wouldn't realize his effect on her — or if he did, he would think it was pain-induced.

'Okay, for modesty's sake, I shall

leave the room while you get into your night things. Once you're in your PJs, I'm coming back to make sure you're comfortable.'

Comfortable? How could she be comfortable with her eye and leg throbbing with pain, her body throbbing with desire and her heart throbbing with love?

Fast as she could, she dragged on her Garfield pajamas and crawled under the covers only seconds before James returned.

He tucked her bedclothes more firmly around her. 'Is your leg okay? Do you want me to raise it up on a pillow?' he asked, looking around for a spare one. 'I could get a cushion from the living room.'

'No, the leg's fine for now.'

'Good.' He sat on the bed. He picked up her hand and held it for a long moment, absently stroking his thumb across her fingers. 'I want to stay and care for you,' he said with quiet deliberation.

169

Fen would have liked nothing better. But no. He would discover her secret. Be strong, Fen, she admonished herself, or all would be lost. 'Thanks for the offer, but I'll be fine. Give my love to Gail and the others.'

'What do you take me for?' He smacked his palm against his thigh in a burst of self-righteous pique. 'I'm not callous. I'll be giving the party a miss.'

'Not on my account,' she protested.

'It was on your account I was going in the first place, sweetheart. Just like Lucinda's. There's no other reason for attending but you.' The spurt of frustration died. He reached over and kissed her on the nose. 'Sleep well, Ms. Grant.'

In spite of the wakeful combination of proximity to James and his kiss, the painkillers began to work and soon Fen fell into a fitful sleep.

She awoke in the early hours of the morning with her leg and hip pounding with excruciating pain. The tablets had worn off. If there was any chance of sleep, she'd have to take more. She tried to get out of bed and stifled a cry as red-hot pokers of pain sliced through her. Tears poured down her cheeks and dripped off her chin.

'Fen, darling?' James was by her side in an instant.

Fen clutched at his body.

'What's up, honey?' he implored her. 'Tell me.'

'Pain . . . need painkillers.' She gave him the name of her strongest ones. 'Need them now,' she gasped out.

He was gone and back in seconds.

Fen swallowed the tablets and allowed James to lay her back on the pillows.

He held her hand and stroked her brow. 'You sure you don't want to go to hospital?' he probed.

Fen couldn't mistake the worried concern in his voice.

'I think it'd be best, darling.'

'I'm never going back there,' she said with a thick grogginess caused by the strong medication. 'Especially not at Christmas.'

James continued caressing Fen's brow with light, gentle strokes. All the while he studied her sleeping form. She was so young and pale and so very vulnerable in her cat pajamas and spiked hair. Her eye was deepening to blues and mauves that had nothing to do with her party make-up. Poor Fen. He wished he could take away her pain.

Fen's breathing became more regular and she slept. James ceased his stroking. He then spent the rest of the night on the floor next to her bed, wrapped in a blanket, in case she needed him.

8

James had to go early next morning. He bristled at leaving Fen alone. She looked terrible with her swollen, blue eye and snow-white cheeks.

But Fen assured him she would ring Trish, her neighbor, if necessary. 'I'm feeling much better,' she insisted. 'I'll be fine. Trish will look after me.'

He didn't like the situation, but Fen was adamant.

Half an hour later, James reached his office, his mood black and morose. It was the last day before Christmas and he had several deals he wanted to get signed, sealed and delivered before everyone shut down for the holiday season.

'You're tetchy this morning,' said Val. 'You're acting like a grumpy bear who's lost his honey pot.'

James huffed and offered as an excuse, 'I didn't sleep much.'

'That's Christmas for you.'

'I wasn't partying.' He filled his mug with coffee from the percolator on the sideboard and loaded it with sugar.

'I see.'

There was a wealth of innuendo behind Valerie Lucas' statement and her grin was saucy, as if she suspected him of extracurricular activities of the adult kind. 'No you don't, Val. I was caring for a sick friend.'

'Very good, King Wenceslas,' she said. 'I'm impressed.'

'Quit the quips. We've a lot of work to get through today. Any messages?'

'Yes, your sister expects you at seven for her drinks party. She also said to remind you you're not allowed to drink because it's your turn to drive everyone to Midnight Mass.'

James inwardly groaned. Another dratted party to endure. 'Great,' he said without a glimmer of enthusiasm.

'And Chrissy Heinz wants you to return her call. She's extending invitations to some Christmas functions.'

This time James groaned aloud. 'Any good news?'

Valerie raised her brows. She was used to the coming and going of women in James' life. 'I don't know. You tell me if this is good news or not. A Fenella Grant rang to say she's going away for Christmas and thank you for last night.' The saucy grin flashed back and she winked. 'So? Good or bad?'

James scowled and pursed his lips.

There was a pregnant pause. 'The jury's out on that one, I see,' and Valerie started to hum *Good King Wenceslas*.

James gave her the evil eye and asked, 'Did Fenella say where she was going?'

'No. I don't usually give your lady friends the third degree.'

Irritation ran over his thoughts. Ms. Grant was being evasive. Again. 'When did she ring?'

'Five minutes before you walked in.'

James snatched up the phone and hit the speed dial.

Valerie waggled her eyebrows as she made her way towards her office. 'I thought we had lots of work to do?'

'We do. But this takes precedence.' He frowned as Fen's answer phone picked up the call. He hung up and called again and again. But either Fen wasn't answering or she had already gone.

Buzzing through to Valerie's office, James asked, 'Val, could you get me Lynette Shaw's number?' He furnished her with the address. 'And make it fast.'

'Yes, boss.'

She came in two minutes later and handed him the number. 'And don't forget to ring Ms. Heinz,' she reminded him.

James called Lynette. Like Fen, she wasn't answering. He'd try again later. He then sighed, pinched the bridge of his nose, sighed again and then reluctantly rang Chrissy.

'Why haven't you called me during the past two weeks?' she demanded.

Her childish petulance irritated James. 'I'm sorry, Chrissy, I've been busy.' He tried to exercise patience. It wasn't her fault he didn't want to see her.

'So have I. I've had all these parties I wanted you to come to but you never returned my calls. I had to go alone.'

'I'm sure you had other friends who could have escorted you.'

'Yes, but that's not the point. I wanted you. I thought we were a couple.'

'Not exclusively, Chrissy. You knew that right from the start.' He drummed his fingers on the desk. The only exclusive dating he wanted was with Fenella Grant.

'But we look good together, James. I prefer dating you to anyone else.'

With determination, he hung on to his patience, fingers drumming a louder and faster tattoo. 'I'm flattered, but I won't be seeing you again. I'm sorry, but I've become involved with someone else, and it's serious.'

'You are kidding, right?'

'No, I mean it. We're over.' He rubbed his tired eyes and wished Chrissy would accept his decision gracefully and end the call.

'You'd dump me for a cripple?'

Her shrill, accusing voice reverberated down the line and made him wince. 'I beg your pardon?' He massaged the back of his stiff and aching neck. Sleeping on Fen's floor and done him no favors, excepting the joy of being close to her. His mind veered back to Fen and her whereabouts. Where the hell had she gone?

Chrissy screeched in his ear. 'You heard me. You'd rather go out with a scarred cripple than a model. You must be losing it, James!'

He stopped massaging. 'What are you going on about?'

'One of my friends said she saw you with that disabled girl from *Cats*.' A harsh laugh sounded. 'I didn't believe them, but I guess it must be true.'

'What disabled girl?' he said in exasperation. 'And I don't know anyone who was in *Cats*. I haven't even seen the show, for goodness sake, and I certainly don't know any dancers.'

'You are such a lousy liar, James. But never mind, when you get fed up with imperfection, you know where to find me. Merry Christmas.'

James stared at the humming receiver, perplexed, and replaced it in its cradle. What was Chrissy going on about? She must have got her wires crossed somewhere along the line. And as for imperfection, nothing was imperfect about his gorgeous Fen.

★　★　★

James was hideously late for his sister's party. He went up the back stairs of Annabelle's house and dumped his coat and suitcase on the bed. He was in no hurry to join the party and so took his time having a long, hot shower before tugging on black jeans and a dark green sweater. When he could delay no longer, he went downstairs.

The drawing room was crowded. There weren't quite so many people as his birthday party, but it was still a sizeable squeeze. Annabelle was addicted to socializing, he decided, and he pitied his long-suffering brother-in-law. There was the summer blonde and one of his aunts, a couple of cousins and several old friends standing around the inglenook fireplace drinking what looked like mulled wine. In a far corner, Lynette and her husband were deep in conversation with the vicar and two elderly women in matching blue twin-sets.

Seeing Lynette lightened his mood considerably. Maybe he would discover how Fen was and where she was staying for Christmas. He desperately wanted to see Fen, hold her, kiss her, love her. James felt displaced without her and very alone. He'd hoped to have contacted Fen and invite her to the party. Or, if she was still suffering from her fall, just stay with her, be close to her.

'James, you've finally made it,' said his sister, giving him a robust kiss and dragging him through the crowd. 'Grab yourself some food. You must be ravenous. And of course, a drink. But only one and not the mulled wine because you're the driver tonight, remember?'

'What's wrong with your famous wine? I was looking forward to sampling some,' said James, casting a glance in the direction of a knot of loudly talking and laughing imbibers.

Annabelle's expression turned smug. 'I think I've excelled myself this year.'

'I see.' And James did. Annabelle's mulled wine was legendary. 'Some other time, then.'

'There's plenty of fruit punch. But get yourself some food first.' Annabelle shoved a plate into his hands.

'Great.'

'Poor baby.' She grinned. 'Dig in and I'll be back later. I've just noticed some more latecomers.'

James stared at the array of cold meats and salads with little interest. Nothing looked appealing.

He replaced the plate on the stack of clean crockery and slipped back out of the room.

In the breakfast room, his nieces were

watching television.

'Hi, Uncle James, come and watch the pretty ladies,' said Claire, the seven-year-old.

'What are you watching?' he asked, ruffling her curls.

'Swan Lake. It's a ballet.'

'Not my scene, kiddo.'

'It's got Auntie Lyn's sister in it,' declared his older niece Ashley. 'She's that one. Odette.' She slipped out of her chair and stabbed a finger at the screen, leaving a sticky smear.

The camera at that moment zoomed in for a close-up. There staring back at him was the beautiful girl he'd seen in the photographs at Fen's flat. Her eyes were large and dark, reflecting the Swan Queen's deep sadness.

He'd seen a pair of eyes very similar just the night before. Fen shared her sister's eyes — endless blue pools of loveliness.

But while the beautiful ballerina exercised an enchanting allure, James wanted his own beautiful Fen. He didn't want to spend Christmas Eve watching her sister dancing on TV. A sister whom he'd never met and hadn't known existed.

He went back to the party and singled out Lynette. 'I've been trying to get hold of Fen all day to find out where she's staying over the holiday period.'

'She's at home, babysitting my terrors.' Lynette grinned. 'I tried to get her to come tonight but she was sensitive about her black eye.'

'Is it a shiner?'

Lynette grinned. 'A beauty.'

'Is she feeling any better after her fall?'

'She's sore,' said Lynette, her gaze flicking away.

'Do you think she'd mind if I joined her babysitting?'

Lynette cocked her head on one side, musingly. Her eyes began to twinkle. 'I think she'd be bowled over.'

Regarding her doubtfully, James said, 'I'll take that as a yes, then.'

'Do.' Lynette hesitated. 'Take our backdoor key. Just let yourself in. Don't bother knocking. You might wake the children.'

James wasted little time driving over to the farm. Snow began to fall as he parked the car in the yard and killed the lights. As quiet as the fat, flakes tumbling from the dark sky, he approached the farmhouse and let himself into the big warm kitchen. He listened. The strains of Swan Lake floated through the house. Fen was watching her sister on the television. It figured. He followed the music to its source.

Stretched out full-length on a floral print couch, Fen's face was bathed in the soft light from the large open fire, fairy lights of the Christmas tree and the glow of the television. But in the dim light, James could make out the floor was covered in scrunched up tissues. The music filled the room; the screen was alive with dancing swans.

Fen broke the spell by blowing her

nose hard and tossing another tissue onto the carpet.

'Fen?'

She shrieked and shot in the air, clutching her chest. 'My God, James! You frightened the life out of me.'

'Sorry, I didn't mean to scare you.'

'How the goodness did you get in?' Fen gabbled like a cornered Christmas turkey facing the axe. 'Are Lynette and Mike with you? I wasn't expecting them home yet. They're usually out ages.' She flicked off the television with the remote control and twisted in her seat, her eyes huge and wary.

'No. Lynette gave me the key and said I could help you babysit. Don't turn the ballet off for me. Carry on.'

'No. It's okay.'

'I don't mind. I know you must want to watch your sister.'

'My sister?' A puzzled crease appeared between her brows.

'Ashley, my niece, told me she was in it. Please, turn it back on.' James shrugged off his overcoat and tossed it

185

onto a nearby armchair. His gaze then alighted on the crutches. 'Crutches? You *did* hurt your leg yesterday.' Guilt washed through him. He shouldn't have listened to her last night but acted on his instincts and taken her to hospital.

'The accident wasn't that bad,' said Fen as she grabbed the TV's remote control.

He watched her fumbling with the controls. She hit a button so a rock'n'roll clip roared on hollering about bats and hell, so she hit another and an old black and white movie flicked on. 'Here, let me.' James sat next to Fen and took the remote controls from her. He flicked through the channels until he relocated Swan Lake.

'We don't have to watch it. It's almost over and I have seen it before. Loads of times.' Her voice sounded reedy.

'Ssh. Enjoy the last act.' James settled an arm around her narrow shoulders and cuddled her to him, dropping a kiss on her cropped hair. He gave a sigh of contentment. At last, he was happy.

★ ★ ★

They sat there in silence. Fen was zinging like a tuning fork, while she could feel James heavy and relaxed next to her.

She barely registered the images on the screen. She was too consumed with panic. How could this be happening? He'd seen her crutches. He was watching her dance. It looked like the final curtain was coming down on her fragile subterfuge. Her stomach churned like an overloaded washing machine.

She was so preoccupied, nibbling her lower lip and working on ways to fox James, she didn't cry like she invariably did when watching one of her old ballet performances. And she didn't realize the credits were rolling until it was too late.

'Turn if off!' she said with uncharacteristic sharpness when she saw them. She lunged for the remote control.

But James dodged her hand and stared transfixed at the screen. 'Fenella

Grant,' he said in a flat tone. 'Fenella Grant?' he repeated, this time sounding puzzled. He turned his head slowly to stare at Fen. 'The Swan Queen was *you!*' His eyes had widened in shocked confusion. The skin was pale and taut around his mouth. Those usually smiley lips were in a grim, harsh line.

Fen gathered her courage. This was one of the hardest moments of her life. She cleared her throat and said a quiet, 'Yes.'

James reacted swiftly, his disbelief still evident in the tense lines of his face and body. He wanted to deny it, she realized. 'But she didn't look like you. Similar, but not quite the same.'

Fen shook her head and tried to lighten the mood to make it easier for James. 'Make-up. Don't you know 'A little bit of powder, a little bit of paint, makes a girl just what she ain't.''

'Oh. I see.'

Fen could tell by his tone he didn't. 'Theatrical make-up changes a person,' she said. 'I could be made to look ninety if the make-up artists put their minds to it.'

His eyes were still wide and confused. 'Why haven't you ever mentioned your dancing? It was obviously a major part of your life. You're famous, for goodness sake!' He waved a hand at the screen.

'Not that famous, James,' she said with what she hoped was crushing scorn. 'Anyway, it's no big deal. I've moved on.'

'Do you still dance?' he asked.

Her throat constricted and she made a superhuman effort to speak through the tightness. 'No.'

'Why?'

What could she say that wouldn't cause a raft of awkward questions? She chose the easiest, most cowardly explanation. 'I'm too old.'

He disclaimed and hugged her. 'You're still a child.'

'Only compared to an ancient forty-year-old.'

'Ouch! You know how to fight dirty.'

The hall clock chimed eleven. James glanced at his watch and groaned. 'Already? I've got to go, I'm afraid, and just when things were getting interesting. I suppose you don't fancy coming to Midnight Mass with me, and then we can carry on this conversation in the car?'

'I'd like nothing better,' Fen lied and hoped her relief at his leaving wouldn't be obvious to him. There were still things she didn't want James finding out. 'But it must have escaped your notice I am here to babysit.'

'Damn, I forgot. I have to go. I promised to take the others to church. My turn to be the skipper this year, otherwise I would ring and cancel it.'

'Both of us have our family responsibilities mapped out for tonight. Such is life.'

'Maybe next year we'll be overlapping them.' He gave her such a tender smile, followed by the longest most lingering kiss ever, that Fen was frightened to wonder what he meant.

As James drove away, she sat by the light of the fire and listened to the throaty roar of the Jensen.

What did he mean by overlapping family responsibilities? Herding all their nieces and nephews into one place and looking after them together?

Or having their very own family unit?

She dropped her head in her hands. She would love nothing more than to marry and have James' babies. He was everything she looked for in a man: strong and sensuous, kind and generous, and with a warm, quirky sense of humor which made his eyes twinkle and mouth curve in his special sexy, contagious smile. He was her soul mate, she was certain of it.

But there was another deep, dark secret she'd kept hidden even from her own sister and parents — the possibility she couldn't carry a child.

Her pelvis had been crushed in the accident. When the car knocked her over, another drove right over her, unable to brake in time. She was lucky to have survived at all. Later the doctors had mentioned the injuries could affect her ability to have a baby.

She knew James adored his sister's children. It was only logical to suppose he would expect to have his own.

If he did, it wouldn't be with her.

She grabbed the tissue box and pulled out the very last one and gave a very big squelchy blow.

★ ★ ★

The old flint-stone church was packed. James and Annabelle, with her husband and children, crammed into one of the back pews. Everyone was rugged up against the cold as the church heaters wheezed out minimal warmth.

'Just made it,' said Annabelle, shivering in her jacket. She was then drawn into a conversation with the family sitting in front of them.

'Did you see the ballet?' Ashley asked the little girl of the family.

'Yes, it was brilliant. Do you think

Mrs. Shaw's sister will teach us how to dance that part if we asked her nicely?'

'No, my mum says she'll never dance again.'

'What's that, Ashley?' interrupted James. 'Why won't she dance again?'

''Cos she's crippled.'

Fen? Crippled? And wasn't that another thing Chrissy had thrown at him? He tried to remember her entire conversation but at the time he hadn't been paying full attention. But Fen crippled? No way. Ashley must be dramatizing. She was so like Annabelle. A right chip off the old block. 'I think you're exaggerating, kiddo,' he said mildly. 'Fen said she was just getting a little old to dance.'

'But she uses crutches,' said his niece.

'Only because she fell over and hurt her leg yesterday,' he said patiently.

'But Mum says she was run over and left for dead.'

'What? When?' Instant, suffocating panic ballooned in his chest. He'd left

193

her safely on the couch, snuggled up by an open fire. She didn't look like someone who'd been run over and left to die in the gutter. He clenched his jaw and was about to race back to Fen, when common sense took over. Fen was okay. Hurt from her fall, but otherwise all right. His panic subsided. 'You had me going there for a second, Ashley,' he said and flicked her cheek.

Ashley wrinkled her nose. 'It happened ages ago, Uncle James.'

He gaped at her. 'When?' But he was silenced by his sister.

'Ssh,' said Annabelle. 'The service is about to start.'

James paid little attention to the service. He joined in the responses and sang the traditional hymns, but his mind was racing, focusing on Fen, trying to slot together all the pieces of the puzzle.

He thought of the time when she'd sounded in so much pain over the phone. He remembered how her friends had assisted her from the nightclub, as had Lynette and Mike from his party. Then there was Lucinda's wacky Christmas speech and Gail's partner's throwaway comment. And he recalled what Fen's friend had said at the same party and her hint there was something about Fen he should know.

So was it this? Was she disabled? If she was, why on earth hadn't she told him? As if he wouldn't have found out. Didn't she trust him? Perhaps she thought it would put him off? No way. He loved her!

As soon as possible, he would confront Ms. Fenella Grant and demand the truth.

★   ★   ★

'You're kidding! You still haven't told him?' Lynette knelt by the Christmas tree surrounded by mountains of torn, brightly patterned wrapping paper which she'd been stowing in a big black plastic sack. She stared at Fen in amazement, her mouth open, her eyebrows high in her hairline, her hands suspended over a pile of paper.

'I wanted to keep it secret,' said Fen. With a defensive hunch of her shoulders, she leaned forward, picking at her red wool dress and avoiding her sister's accusing expression. 'You know that, Lynny.'

'Yes, but you've been spending so much time with him, I presumed he knew. He's been talking to Annabelle about buying a property around here and maybe starting his own little dynasty.' She shook her head. 'I thought it was because of you.'

Oh God! Fen closed her eyes in despair. He *had* been thinking of happy families.

Fen hung her head. The realization made her feel worse. When Annabelle had given James' particulars for the Discreet Liaison's files, she had mentioned he was fatally shy of commitment and had no intention of settling down. Well, hadn't James come a long way in a few weeks! Now he talked of marriage and babies — with a woman who was a cripple and unable to give him what he wanted. The whole thing was sickeningly pathetic. How had she let it get this far? She should have cancelled his membership from day one and avoided any further contact. But no, she hadn't, and the result was a mess.

'I can't see how you've kept it secret,' said Lynette as she half-heartedly resumed her tidying, her brow still furrowed.

Fen couldn't blame her for wondering. 'I didn't say it had been easy.'

'Good grief.' Lynette's eyes widened and she stopped mid-thrust with a ball of paper in her hand. 'What's he going to say when he finds out?'

'Why the hell didn't you tell me, that's what,' said James, his voice coming from the doorway.

Fen yelped and her heart yammered hard against her ribs. Dread uncurled in her belly and crawled through her bloodstream.

James gave her a tight smile and then

transferred his attention to Lynette. 'Merry Christmas, ladies. I hope you don't mind me intruding. Mike said it would be okay.'

'Of course it's okay. You're always welcome. Do come and sit down while I go and help Mike with some drinks.' Lynette scrambled to her feet and bounded towards the door.

James side-stepped to let her pass and then continued to stand in the doorway. 'Not going to come over here and welcome me, Fen? Fling your arms around my neck and wish me Merry Christmas under the mistletoe?' He waved a hand at the sprig in the arch above his head.

Fen worried her bottom lip and wished the couch would morph into a giant fish, swallow her up and take her out to sea and away from this agonizingly awkward scene.

'Well?' There was steel behind the question.

'You know I can't,' she said flatly.

'Only by default, thanks to my

ten-year-old ballet-mad niece. When were you planning on telling me?' His voice rose. 'Soon? Sometime? Never!'

Fen wrapped her arms around her small frame and sucked her lip some more. Ice filled her veins where once warm blood had flowed. She was frozen in her unhappiness. What could she say to make it any better between them? She'd betrayed them both because of her own sense of pride. She couldn't blame James for being mad because she was mad at herself, and at fate, for dealing her such a hand.

'Didn't you think I'd notice? God, do you take me for a fool, Fen?'

'No.' All she could manage was a whisper.

'So why the big smokescreen?'

'I had my reasons.'

'Which were?' He flung off his coat and strode up and down the length of the room, kicking at the waste wrapping paper. His brows were drawn together in a deep frown, a pulse hammered in his cheek and his mouth was a thin, straight line. He picked up her two crutches and stared at them, his lip curling in disgust. Fen's nephew had tied tinsel on each crutch for a humorous festive touch. He threw them away from him.

Fen winced, dread heavy in her stomach. He looked so scrumptious in his black jeans and green sweater, his hair curling from the damp weather. She yearned to run to him and envelop him in her arms, tell him she hadn't meant to hurt him, that she would love him always.

But she couldn't.

He wanted a family and she wasn't the one to provide it.

Best to let him go now, before they got in any deeper.

9

'Tell me, Fen. Help me understand.' James took two long strides towards Fen and squatted in front of her. He reached for her upper arms and held her firm, staring deep into her eyes. 'Tell me. I need to know.'

She ducked her head and, with halting, half finished sentences, told him about the accident and the months of lying in a hospital bed, the operations and endless, grueling physiotherapy. She spared him nothing and watched his expression softening as she spoke.

'You poor darling,' he said, and he gathered her to him so Fen could nestle into his secure warmth. 'But why have you kept me in the dark about it? Didn't you think I'd care? That I wouldn't understand?'

Fen raised her head and recognized the empathetic pain in his eyes, witnessed the pity shining out of them, and her heart sank. 'Because of what I see in your face,' she said with tragic simplicity.

James pulled back from her. 'What do you mean? What do you see?' Hurt laced his words.

Fen shrugged and said with quiet dignity, 'Pity. I've had my fill of compassion and pity. Of people treating me as if I'm a strange fragile creature who mustn't be upset.'

James opened his mouth to remonstrate, but Fen held her finger over his warm lips, enjoying the feel of him, savoring it. Today could be the last time she would touch him in such an intimate way.

'Let me finish, James. I know it's sad. I know I've lost my career. I wish I could run and dance and walk without my damn crutches. But I can't. But I am getting stronger. I will regain more mobility given time. The bottom line is I can feel sorry for myself, but I don't want others feeling obliged to be sorry for me. It's nothing to do with them.

'When you came on the scene, you treated me as an equal. You didn't know I was crippled. You yelled at me, insulted me, laughed with me, kissed me, and all because you thought I was perfectly normal and could handle it. You don't know how precious that was. A lot of people are put off by my injuries. They're disgusted. Disability makes them feel uncomfortable.'

James cursed but Fen ignored him.

'I didn't want to put you off until the last possible moment. I knew all about your Gorgeous Gazelles, those perfect young women who were models or actresses or simply beautiful creatures, whom you constantly dated. I knew I couldn't compete with them.'

She sighed and swallowed against a burning throat. 'It was very hard keeping my disability secret, but I selfishly wanted to enjoy our friendship on an equal level for as long as possible. I'm sorry if I've hurt you or disappointed you. I didn't mean to. I hope you can forgive me.'

James flung himself away and resumed his frustrated pacing of the room. He ran his fingers through his hair, rumpling it to within an inch of its life, and then shoved his hands deep into his pockets and glared at Fen.

'I can't believe you'd shut me out of such an important part of your life,' he bit out, the anger back in full force. 'Forgive you? I can forgive you for trying to protect me from what you perceive to be unpleasantness. But I take issue with the fact that you'd think I would be so crass as to not date you because you can't walk unaided. It doesn't disgust me you need crutches, Fen. It's just another facet of you.' He stalked up and down the room for several tense seconds and then declared, 'And for the record, I don't only date models and actresses!'

'When was the last time you didn't, James?' she asked and waited, wondering what he would say. They both knew his track record.

James opened and shut his mouth. He frowned as he thought about it. A wariness sprung into his eyes and Fen waited patiently as he confronted his past. And then his expression cleared and turned smug. 'Okay, Lucinda and Gail, not including you.'

Fen could have laughed out loud if it wasn't so sad. 'But you only dated us because of Discreet Liaisons,' she pointed out.

'I didn't intentionally set out to date models.' His chin jerked up in a defensive tilt, challenging her to deny it. 'It just happened that way.'

'Well, you've slummed it with us Discreet Liaison girls long enough. It's time you picked up with your Gorgeous Gazelles again.'

'Will you stop using that phrase!' he said as he jammed a hand through his hair.

'I think it's very appropriate. It was a stroke of genius when Annabelle coined it.'

'Annabelle's only stroke of genius

was to introduce me to you!' He swung around and hauled her into his arms. He sat back down on the couch with Fen cradled in his lap.

'I'm not hurting you?' he said anxiously as Fen sucked in a breath and winced as her sore limbs protested.

Fen struck him on the shoulder. 'See. There you go. If you hadn't known about my accident you wouldn't have cared two hoots if I hurt or not. You would have just picked me up and be damned.'

'Actually, I would have checked. I know you had a bad fall two nights ago. That would have been enough to arouse my concern. You were in a bad way, sweetheart.'

'Hmph.'

'But I'm not going to ask you if it's all right to kiss you.' With that his mouth descended on hers and he kissed her with satisfying thoroughness.

When they came up for air, James said, 'I've wanted to kiss you ever since I arrived today.'

'And very nice it was too,' said Fen with a deep sigh. She snuggled closer to him even though she knew she would have to stop. Their relationship was doomed to fail. 'But — '

'No buts, Fen.'

'Yes there is, James. A big, ugly important one we need to discuss before we go any further.'

'We'll talk about it later. Not now. Kiss me instead.' He cupped his hands around her face and regarded her tenderly. 'I love you, Fenella Grant.'

Fen felt herself drowning in his loving gaze and allowed herself the indulgence of one more kiss. And then another . . .

Lynette knocked and came crashing into the room. 'Oops, sorry. Do I need the fire extinguisher or is it safe to come in?' She flapped her hand in front of her face and grinned.

'Just,' said James, raising his head from Fen's and grinning back.

'Good. Mum and Dad are here and lunch is almost ready. I wondered if you'd like to stay and join us, James?'

'I'd love to, if there's enough to go around.'

There was plenty and James joined in the rowdy lunch, sitting next to Fen. He enjoyed having her close so he could just reach out and touch her and link his fingers with hers. She was a little quiet, but he presumed it was the fall-out from their emotional exchange. As for him, he was feeling great. He was with the woman he loved. There were no more secrets between them. Life was fantastic.

Towards the end of the meal, Lynette handed out Christmas crackers, which were festive table novelties made of brightly colored paper and foil. They contained trinkets, jokes and paper hats and made a small bang when pulled apart. Much laughter ensued as Ashley won a false mustache, her mother a fake finger and her grandfather a pink whistle in the shape of a parrot.

When it came to James' turn, he won a green plastic ring. He picked it up

208

and stared at it for a few seconds, feeling the rush of blood to his head and heart. The ring was a sign. His throat convulsed at the enormity of what he now intended to do and he sucked in a steadying breath. Slipping his arm around Fen's shoulders, he leaned towards her and whispered, 'Fenella Grant, will you marry me?'

'Marry you?' Fen gasped, her eyes widening in dismay. Her cheeks flushed rose-pink and then bleached.

'I know it's not a diamond ring, but I'll buy you one just as soon as the shops are open. Promise,' he smiled, holding the green ring between his finger and thumb.

The family members around the table fell silent. Everyone held his or her breath.

Fen squirmed in embarrassment.

James watched the struggle of emotions warring across her pale face. There was dismay, pain, sadness, but no joy.

She clenched her hands together and

looked wide-eyed towards him. 'I told you,' she whispered through pinched lips. 'There's an important 'but'.'

'And I told you we could deal with it,' he said, his voice low to match hers.

'Stop whispering together like a couple of love-struck teenagers,' declared Lynette. 'Are you intending to keep us in suspense?'

'Lynette,' admonished her mother. 'Marriage is not a matter to be taken lightly.' But she stared intently at Fen, waiting.

'Say yes, Auntie Fen,' piped up her niece.

'Do say yes,' added Lynette, ignoring her mother's frown of disapproval and giving her daughter the thumbs up sign.

'Lynette!' said her mother again.

James ignored them. His focus was on Fen, who looked stricken and trapped. 'I love you, Fen, for better or for worse, in sickness and in health. Marry me!'

'If I wasn't a damn cripple,' she cried out, 'I would walk out of here with my head held high. Instead I have to sit here while we both suffer the embarrassment of me declining you.'

James felt he'd been struck, but then he saw tears pooling in Fen's eyes. He realized she hadn't turned him down because she didn't love him. She had refused him because she did.

He scraped back his chair and threw his linen serviette onto the table. 'You want to leave the room, sweetheart, then we'll leave it. Excuse us, everyone.' He slipped the ring in his pocket, pulled back Fen's chair and scooped her into his arms.

'Put me down,' she said, her body taut, her eyes large and dark and haunted with misery.

'Not until you tell me everything.' He strode into the living room, kicked the door shut with his foot and laid her on the couch. He then stood tall and brooding, staring down at her, his hands stuffed in his jean pockets and his face set. 'Talk to me, Fenella. Tell me what I'm missing, what I need to know.'

'I can't marry you,' she said in a whisper.

'Because you're crippled?' He gave a snort. 'I love you, regardless of whether or not you can walk. I love you. All of you. Don't you understand?' Frustration bit deep. What could he say to her that would convince her of his sincerity? Would make her change her mind?

'Yes. But *you* don't understand. I don't think I can have children. My pelvic injuries were so severe. I need to have tests. To find out if . . . if . . . ' Her words tumbled over themselves in her effort to spit out the depressing facts. Tears shimmered and clung to her lashes.

James continued to stare down at her, forcing her to confront her self-erected barriers that were keeping them apart. 'So?'

'But you want a family, James!'

'Yes, but I want you more than I want a family.' He ached to touch her but knew he had to finish. 'I want you as my family. I only want you. I need

212

you.' His voice cracked unashamedly. 'Only you, darling Fen.'

'But James, Annabelle said you've been talking of establishing your own dynasty.'

'I love her dearly, but Annabelle talks too much and often misses the point.'

'But — '

'Fen.' James held up one hand to silence her. In the other hand he held the green plastic cracker ring. He dropped on one knee, took her small pale hand in his and asked, 'Will you marry me?'

She stared deep into his eyes and saw the love and sincerity radiating from them. How could she refuse him? She loved him more than life itself. If he didn't care about her infirmities, then why should she? 'Yes,' she whispered, her voice tremulous with joy.

'Thank God for that.' Raw emotion shook his own voice. He'd nearly lost her, but now she was his, his own darling girl. James then fitted the ring on her finger and kissed her nose. 'Now let's go back and put an end to Lynette's suspense. Though first I'm going to kiss you thoroughly. We both deserve it.' His lips came down on hers with a sure, firm boldness that was coupled with warm, sensuous promise and left them both breathless and lightheaded by the time the kiss ended.

James then picked her up and Fen wound her arms around his neck. 'I love you, Mr. McAllister,' she said with simple sincerity.

'I love you too, Ms. Grant.' And he kissed her again for several long, throbbing moments before succumbing to duty and carrying her back into the dining room.

As they stepped into the room, the family's conversation stopped. Expectant gazes were turned towards the rumpled but grinning couple.

Fen held her hand aloft to show off her green plastic engagement ring and her family erupted into noisy congratulations.

'Thank goodness for that,' said

Lynette, wiping her moist eyes, her smile almost as wide as Fenella's. 'I think this deserves a toast. Here's to the happy couple.' She held her glass high.

One of the children let off a party-popper, which prompted the others to follow suit until there was a hail of bangs and streamers gaudily wreathing the table, chairs and family.

'Not just happy, we're ecstatic,' declared James. His gaze met Fen's and his heart flipped and dipped at her shining countenance. All traces of doubt and hurt had been wiped away in the sure flood of their love. 'Isn't that right?' he whispered, bending towards her and tenderly kissing her soft lips.

'Oh, yes, my love.' And she kissed him back wholeheartedly.

THE END

SINISTER ISLE OF LOVE

Phyllis Mallett

Jenny Carr is joining her brother on the Caribbean island of Taminga to start a new life. On her way, she meets Peter Blaine, a successful businessman on the island. He couldn't be more of a contrast to Craig Hannant, whose business is failing. His wife had died in mysterious circumstances, and Craig is now a difficult man to be around — but Jenny falls for Craig, despite all the signs that she is making the biggest mistake of her life . . .

CUPID'S BOW

Toni Anders

When romantic novelist Janey first meets Ashe Corby, she is not impressed. But frustratingly, the hero in the latest novel she is writing persists in resembling him! As Janey gets to know Ashe, she comes to admire and like him. But when she attempts to help Ashe's son Daniel to realise his dream of studying horticulture, Ashe is furious at what he sees as interference on Janey's part. Miserable without each other, will love win through for them?

MISTLETOE MEDICINE

Anna Ramsay

Ever since he wrecked her romance with Dickie Derby, Nurse Hannah Westcott has harboured a thorough dislike of Dr Jonathan Boyd-Harrington — but she never expected to see him again. To her horror, he turns up as Senior Registrar at the Royal Hanoverian Hospital, and there is no way she can avoid him — especially when he takes an interest in the hospital panto. Hannah has the star part, but it would seem she must play Nurse Beauty to Jonathan Boyd-Harrington's Dr Beast . . .

LEAP YEAR

Marilyn Fountain

Tired of the city rush, Erin Mallowson takes a twelve-month lease on Owl Cottage in Norfolk to run her own image consultancy business. Her ex-boss and commitment-phobic boyfriend Spencer thinks she's mad. Keen to embrace the village lifestyle, Erin doesn't expect it to include the enigmatic Brad Cavill, a former footballer with a troubled past. But even though work and love refuse to run smoothly, it turns out to be a leap year that Erin never wants to end . . .

PRAIRIE ROSE

Catriona McCuaig

1912. Working as a schoolteacher on the Canadian prairie, Paula Scott is courted by Jake Marriott, the father of one of her pupils. Her friends consider him a good catch, but Paula is secretly in love with Charles Ingram. Charles, however, is engaged to selfish society beauty Lola King. Paula knows she must forget Charles, but would it be fair to wed Jake when he can only be second best in her heart?

FLAMES THAT MELT

Angela Britnell

Tish Carlisle returns from Tennessee to clear out her late father's house in Cornwall — to several surprises. The first is the woman and baby she discovers living there and the second is her father's solicitor, Nico De Burgh, who was Tish's first love. Nico fights their renewed attraction because of a promise made to his foster father but Tish won't give up on him. They must share their secrets before they have any chance of a loving future together . . .